KU-031-550

She breathed in—this time a long, slow, delicious breath, which not only absorbed Marco's scent, but also the firmness of his chest, the warmth of his skin, and the loud and solid sound of his beating heart.

His fingers, which had gently held her with perfect stillness, started moving against her skin with feather-soft touches.

Heat built.

She gasped as his heart jumped to match hers, sending vibrations of unambiguous wanting—his wanting—into every cell of her body. His body called to hers, urging a response, but the call was unnecessary. Her body was already throbbing to the beat of his.

What are you doing?

With a gut-dropping shock, she realised exactly what she was doing. *Oh, God.* Not only weren't his arms a place of safety and protection—they had *Danger* written all over them.

Dear Reader

A couple of years ago I was fortunate enough to attend a polo match. Watching those nuggety polo ponies strut their stuff was awe-inspiring. With their hogged (roached) manes and braided tails, they have amazing agility and can turn on the spot. Polo players will tell you that their game is eighty percent horse and twenty percent their own skill.

Ever since that sunny Saturday afternoon I have wanted to have a polo match in a book, but each story ended up on a different trajectory and the polo match didn't fit. Until now. I mean how could I have a gorgeous Argentine hero and *not* have a polo match?

However, I didn't realise how important this polo match would be to my characters until I wrote the book and the polo match became another character in the story.

Marco is from Argentina and living in Outback Australia. He answered the call to come to Australia to help fill the doctor shortage, and now he is there his greatest wish is to stay and carve out a life for himself and his young son, who has mild cerebral palsy.

Lucy Patterson grew up in Bulla Creek, Western Australia, the much-loved only child of the local doctor. In keeping with family tradition Lucy became a doctor, and had plans to join her father—until her mother died and her world was turned upside down.

I'll let the book tell their story. Meanwhile, if you want to see the pictures and videos that inspired the book head to www.fionalowe.com. I love to hear from my readers, and you can find me on Facebook, Twitter and Goodreads.

Happy Reading!

Love

Fiona xx

LETTING GO WITH DR RODRIGUEZ

BY
FIONA LOWE

All the characters in this book have no existence outside the imagination of the author, and have no relation whatsoever to anyone bearing the same name or names. They are not even distantly inspired by any individual known or unknown to the author, and all the incidents are pure invention.

All Rights Reserved including the right of reproduction in whole or in part in any form. This edition is published by arrangement with Harlequin Enterprises II BV/S.à.r.l. The text of this publication or any part thereof may not be reproduced or transmitted in any form or by any means, electronic or mechanical, including photocopying, recording, storage in an information retrieval system, or otherwise, without the written permission of the publisher.

® and TM are trademarks owned and used by the trademark owner and/or its licensee. Trademarks marked with ® are registered with the United Kingdom Patent Office and/or the Office for Harmonisation in the Internal Market and in other countries.

First published in Great Britain 2012
by Mills & Boon, an imprint of Harlequin (UK) Limited.
Large Print edition 2013
Harlequin (UK) Limited, Eton House,
18-24 Paradise Road, Richmond, Surrey TW9 1SR

© Fiona Lowe 2012

ISBN: 978 0 263 23083 3

Harlequin (UK) policy is to use papers that are natural, renewable and recyclable products and made from wood grown in sustainable forests. The logging and manufacturing process conform to the legal environmental regulations of the country of origin.

Printed and bound in Great Britain
by CPI Antony Rowe, Chippenham, Wiltshire

Always an avid reader, **Fiona Lowe** decided to combine her love of romance with her interest in all things medical, so writing Medical Romance™ was an obvious choice! She lives in a seaside town in southern Australia, where she juggles writing, reading, working and raising two gorgeous sons with the support of her own real-life hero!

Recent books by the same author:

SYDNEY HARBOUR HOSPITAL:
   TOM'S REDEMPTION*
CAREER GIRL IN THE COUNTRY
SINGLE DAD'S TRIPLE TROUBLE
THE MOST MAGICAL GIFT OF ALL
HER BROODING ITALIAN SURGEON
MIRACLE: TWIN BABIES

Sydney Harbour Hospital

**These books are also available in eBook format
from www.millsandboon.co.uk**

NORFOLK LIBRARY AND
INFORMATION SERVICE
SUPPLIER   MAGNA
INVOICE No. IO64686
ORDER DATE 28-1-13
COPY No.   SIO

For Monica, with thanks
for giving my eldest son
an amazing time in France, and for
all her help with Marco's Spanish.

Special thanks to Alan,
who cheerfully answered my e-mail
and gave me a rundown on the
intricacies of visas.

CHAPTER ONE

'LUCE, wait.'

Dr Lucy Patterson heard the call and with a smile, she thrust her hand against the fast-closing elevator doors at Perth City Hospital. They bounced open.

A moment later, Daniel Edgerton, radiographer and her boyfriend, strode over the silver threshold. 'Thanks.' His smile for her wasn't quite as broad as it had been in the past, but if he was as weary as she was, she totally understood.

He slapped the large 'G' button with the heel of his hand. 'You finishing up for the day?'

She bit her lip, knowing he wasn't going to be thrilled with her reply. 'Not quite. I have to admit a late addition to the prof's surgical list and re-site an IV.'

His sigh reverberated around the boxed space, settling over her with cloying disapproval. He worked a roster with a definite start and end time, and he didn't always understand that her day finished when the work was finally complete. With forced brightness and a wide smile, she quickly added, 'But then I'll be done and yours for the night.'

Daniel opened his mouth but an ominous grinding sound drowned out his reply and the smooth descent of the elevator suddenly jerked, throwing Lucy sideways.

She gripped the support rail and righted herself. 'Please, no, not again. I got stuck here last week for twenty minutes.'

'It's not a total disaster.' Daniel reached his arm around her waist, pulling her in close and nuzzling her neck as he ran his hand up her back, his fingers reaching for her bra strap. 'We can do a lot with twenty minutes.'

She laughed, but splayed her fingers against his chest, leaning back and putting some distance between them. 'True, but I'm not risking my senior registrar's application by being caught "in flagrante" in an elevator.'

His blue eyes hardened as he dropped his arms to his sides. 'Jess didn't have a problem with it.'

She blinked at him in surprise. Jess was her

house-mate of four years and they got along well, sharing not only a house but gossip, clothes and after a tough day, a glass of wine. 'There's no way Jess would have sex in an elevator.'

He shrugged—the action a total disregard of her reply. 'There's every way and she did.'

A jab of indignation caught Lucy under the ribs and she crossed her arms. 'If Jess had sex in an elevator she'd have told me.'

Daniel's brows rose as his mouth flattened. 'She doesn't have to tell you everything, Luce, and let's face it, just lately you've hardly been around.'

Lucy stifled a flicker of unease that Jess may have confided in Dan rather than her. 'Why are you so certain she did?'

This time Daniel crossed his arms. 'Because I was there.'

'You were there?' Confusion drove the words across her lips and for the briefest moment she thought Daniel meant he'd walked in on Jess and her lover when the elevator doors had opened. Suddenly, her sluggish brain decoded his body language—stiff and defiant—and a chill raced through her so hard and fast that she trembled.

'*You* had sex with Jess?' Her voice rose and cracked. 'Here?'

He met her shocked gaze with a combative glare. 'Yeah.'

Her friend. Her hand flew to her mouth as nausea spun her stomach and threatened to return the chocolate muffin she'd just eaten. Stepping back, she flattened herself against the wall and tried to put as much distance between them as possible. 'When?'

Dan sucked in his lips and finally said, 'Last week.'

She thought back to the sex they'd had last Wednesday after she'd cooked his favourite dinner—the night she'd been the one making all the moves. At the time it had surprised her because usually Dan initiated sex, but it hadn't taken long before he'd got on board. Her stomach pitched again. Desperately trying to keep her composure, she spoke softly but with an edge of steel. '*When* last week?'

For the first time, he dropped his gaze. 'It doesn't matter.'

She gripped the support rail as her knees turned to jelly. 'Yes, it bloody matters.'

He ran his hand over his short-cropped hair. 'Look, Luce, there's no point—'

'Tell me!' She heard her tears in the shout as she lost the battle to hold herself together.

'Wednesday afternoon.'

It was as if the cable of the elevator snapped right there and then, releasing the silver box into free-fall. Only it was her life that was tumbling and crashing down around her, and taking all the supporting pillars with it. Pillars she'd barely shored up after they'd spectacularly collapsed in on her six months ago, making her question everything she'd ever believed in.

Every part of her was numb—her lungs refused to move and tears blurred her eyes. How could this be happening? Why now when everything else in her life, including her career, was so unsettled? A shot of righteous anger suddenly pierced through the numbness giving rise to blessed pain. 'You bastard.'

His head snapped up. 'Oh, that's rich. I'm the bastard, but you've been the one who's been closed off for months. You might be standing next to me, but you're never really here. Jess at least understands me. Jess gives me something. You've given me nothing for way too long, Lucy.'

Her anger swelled, propelled by a hammering heart and utter devastation. 'You're not just a bastard, Dan, you're a selfish bastard. You know what's been going on with me and Da—' She stopped herself, not able to finish that particular word. She swallowed and pushed on. 'With William. You know what I've been going through, but that doesn't count for anything, does it? Nothing matters if it's not all about you.'

His mouth tightened giving his boyish face a hard edge. 'It's been all about you for months, Luce, and I've had enough.'

She'd known in her heart things weren't good between them, but she'd never expected such a bitter betrayal. 'Then why didn't you just leave? Why take my friend with you?'

A light came into his eyes. 'I think I love her.'

The simple words plunged into her heart making her double up in pain. Words he'd never voiced to her in all their time together. Her chest rose and fell way too fast and she put her hands around her mouth so she didn't hyperventilate.

Daniel slammed his hands against the 'door

open' button. 'Come on.' He hit every other button too, wanting out of this box of torrid emotions as much as she did.

Lucy dug deep and found her voice. 'You say you love Jess and yet you still had sex with me? Oh, that's classy, Dan, really classy.' The combined infidelity of her friends burned through her soul. 'You both deserve each other.'

A trace of contrition played across his cheeks. 'Look, Luce, I'm sorry it ended this way, but it's not *all* my fault.'

Utter wretchedness dragged at her and she nodded mutely, not because she agreed with him, but because she couldn't voice even a tenth of her feelings at the utter disloyalty of the two people she'd drawn on for support over most of the year.

A whirring noise sounded, followed by the elevator moving slowly down. Finally the doors opened with a ping and Daniel muttered, 'Thank God,' before stepping out and walking away without a backwards glance.

The doors slid shut and Lucy sank to the floor, closing her eyes. Even in her darkest moments she'd never imagined she would have been part of the conversation that had just taken place. She lurched from one memory to another, searching for clues, hints—anything at all that might have prepared her for Daniel's bombshell. Things had been strained, but there'd been no hint of him and Jess.

None that you noticed. But then again, you haven't noticed much lately, have you?

Her head pounded and resentment burned through her. She felt her smart-phone vibrate and she pulled it out of the deep pocket in her white coat, expecting a message from the ward asking where she was and how much longer she'd be, because her patient was overdue for IV antibiotics. The message wasn't from the ward, but an email from an unfamiliar name.

She squinted through her headache to make the words come into focus.

Ms Patterson,

As you know, your father, Dr William Patterson, has fractured his tibia. He is not a man to ask for help so I, as his doctor and the second medical practitioner in Bulla Creek, am asking for you to visit at your earliest convenience.

Marco Rodriguez (Dr)

She stared at the email, reading it three times before the words finally sank in. *Fractured tibia?* She bit her lip as guilt spun around worry. Of course she hadn't known about William's leg. She hadn't communicated with him in months and the emails he'd sent had dealt only with the information she'd requested. None had mentioned his health. Neither had he mentioned a doctor with a Spanish name and a formal writing style, which indicated that English wasn't his native language. What was a Spaniard doing in outback Bulla Creek?

At your earliest convenience. She instinctively shook her head and then, from the tangled mess that was currently her life, she stared up at the ceiling of the elevator absolutely certain about one thing. No way was she going back to Bulla Creek.

You mean home.

'No, I mean Bulla Creek.' Her emphatic voice sounded strident in the confines of the otherwise empty elevator.

Right, so you're ignoring duty, staying in Perth where your boyfriend's just dumped you, and your housemate has utterly betrayed you. That's gonna be cosy. Kinda makes Bulla Creek almost attractive, doesn't it?

Lucy dropped her head in her hands and wished she could wind back the clock one year—back to a time when she knew who she was, knew where she belonged and where she was headed. Instead she now faced a road that stretched way out in front of her that was filled with a pea-soup fog.

Every part of her railed against the idea of going back to Bulla Creek, but the news about William tore at the box she'd shoved all her feelings about him into—feelings she didn't want to revisit. They came back anyway in unsettling waves. No matter what had happened between them and no matter how much she didn't want to see him, she couldn't just ignore the fact he'd broken his leg. Not at his age. The doctor in her knew that only too well. Acknowledging it smoothed out her tangled thoughts.

'I'll take some annual leave, fly up to Bulla Creek for a quick visit and check that William's receiving the correct medical care. Then I'll come back here, find a new place to live and sort out the rest of my life, which won't include disloyal friends and cheating, bastard men.'

You do realise there isn't anyone here listening except me and I don't need to hear you talk to know exactly what you're thinking.

'Shut-up.' The yell propelled Lucy to her feet and she brushed down her white coat. Her life was in tatters, but at least she had a plan. One she was clinging to like a floating log in a choppy sea.

The red dust of Bulla Creek was covered in a layer of green, courtesy of a record-setting wet winter followed by a sunny spring. The sheep wore thick fleeces, lambs gambolled on fat legs and the farmers smiled, which was almost as uncommon as the weather. Dr Marco Rodriguez returned a farmer's hat tip and grin as he strode down the main street toward the Bulla Creek Medical Centre. It wasn't the first time he'd reflected on the fact that, in general, farmers in Western Australia shared a taciturn approach to life that was very similar to that of the farmers of his homeland of Argentina. Life on the land was tough and a good season was cause for celebration.

He turned left at the rust-and-sand-coloured

church, which stood diagonally opposite the pub. Both buildings had been built over a hundred years ago from local rocks quarried when veins of lead in the nearby hills had guaranteed prosperity. Bulla Creek today was not as affluent as it had been back then, but the legacy of heritage buildings not only reminded residents of its wealthy past, but more importantly it brought in tourists with money to spend. People paid a lot to step back in time and spend a weekend or longer imagining simpler times.

Marco knew it was just an illusion. There'd been nothing simple about living without running water and basic hygiene in a time when a broken leg had often resulted in amputation, when the birth of a child could easily take the life of a mother and a secondary infection after a common cold could kill. Even today, childbirth had its risks and he was far too intimate with the dangers.

Pulling open the door of the modern medical clinic, which also fronted a small hospital annexe of five acute-care beds and ten nursing-home beds, he walked into a packed waiting room. Just as he'd done every day for the last few weeks since his medical partner had fallen ill. He was worried about William who'd been adamant he didn't want his daughter told about his accident, although when he spoke of her his eyes lit up before sadness filled them.

William was not his usual, upbeat self and he was taking longer to return to work than expected. With the death of his wife earlier in the year and now the fracture, Marco believed he needed cheering up.

He pressed down on the ripple of unease that had been trickling through him ever since he'd overridden the other doctor's request and written to William's daughter. He'd needed to do something because he really believed William needed time with family so he could re-find his spark. With one doctor down, Marco's days ran together in a long blur of work with snatches of fatherhood wedged in between. This wasn't what he'd envisaged when he'd made the decision to come to Bulla Creek. It was supposed to have meant more time for Ignacio, not less. He needed William back at work yesterday.

He swallowed a sigh and mustered up a smile for his waiting patients because his problems were not theirs and they deserved his complete attention. '*Buenos días*. Good morning, everyone. I am at your service in just a few moments.'

'We have an empty waiting room and I'm off home. You should go too while you can.'

Marco looked up from reading pathology reports to see Sue Hogarth, practice nurse, farmer's wife and soon-to-be grandmother, standing in the doorway of his office. 'Ten minutes more.'

She nodded slowly. 'I'll lock up the front doors then and all you have to do is go out the back and make sure it's locked behind you.'

'Sure. Thank you for your help today.'

'Ah, Marco, that all Australian men could be so polite. See you tomorrow when we get to do it all again.' She grinned and pushed off the architrave preparing to leave, but turned back suddenly. 'Oh, Ignacio's appointment's been changed to Tuesday. I've put it directly into your electronic calendar. Night.'

'Goodnight.' He heard her fading footsteps and the door slam shut. He waited a moment and then smiled as he soaked up the peace of a closed clinic—silent phones, still rooms and the blissful quiet of absolutely no interruptions. He finished reading the reports, methodically listing the names of the patients that Sue needed to call tomorrow to schedule review appointments, and as he reached the last one he let out a breath. Thankfully there were no sinister results in this batch and he was spared the need to make the hard phone call and give someone seriously bad news. He hated doing that as it reminded him of the time he'd received it and the powerlessness that came with it.

He texted Heather—his housekeeper and Ignacio's afterschool caregiver—telling her he'd be home in ten minutes and then he packed up his desk. Grabbing his bag, he entered the corridor and headed toward the back door, flicking off the hall lights as he reached the switch. The expected darkness didn't come. With a sigh, he realised that Sue had left the office light on and he spun on his heel, walking the length of the corridor to turn it off.

As he slid his hand up the doorway to reach the switch, something made him glance into the room. A round and pert, jeans-clad bottom stared straight at him. '*Querido Dios.*' Shocked surprise sent his English scurrying and it took a moment for him to find the correct words. 'What are you *doing*?'

A young woman turned abruptly from the computer, her chin-length, chestnut-red hair swinging wildly around her guilt-streaked face. Round eyes, the colour of an Argentine summer sky just before the descent of a storm, stared at him, brimming with a thousand emotions. A heartbeat later they cleared as if she was practised in forcing her feelings to retreat until only defiance remained. She stood less than tall despite the boost of high wedge heels and then her chin tilted up, her shoulders rolled back and her breasts rose, straining against the free-flowing pink halter top that draped itself around her curves and ended by softly caressing her hips.

A jolt of heat whipped him—heat that hadn't flared in his veins for a long time—and for the briefest of moments his eyes followed the tantalising fall of the soft material as if they hoped to glimpse what nestled behind it. Thankfully, common sense shot in to rescue him and he quickly hauled his gaze back to her face.

At that precise moment he knew the words he should have spoken were 'Who are you?'

As if reading his mind she stepped forward, extending her hand. 'You must be Marco Rodriguez. I'm Lucy.'

The overly wide smile gave her away. From the age of fourteen girls had flirted with him, and it had taken him almost as long to learn that the flirting wasn't always about wanting him. Often it was about wanting something else entirely—a bitter lesson that Bianca had taught him too well. Now at thirty-three, his radar was pretty well tuned. She spoke as if he should recognise her, using his name as a bridge to connect them with a familiarity that didn't exist. He had an excellent memory and he knew they'd not met before.

You would have remembered those breasts.

He shrugged away the inconvenient awakening of his libido and focused on the facts. He might not know her but he did know that whoever she was, she shouldn't be here in an office that didn't belong to her. Neither should she be viewing a computer that contained the confidential files of all of the patients of Bulla Creek and the surrounding district.

A fizz of anger shook him and for the first time in a long, long time his inherent good manners deserted him. He didn't greet her and instead left her extended hand hovering between them.

Damn it. Lucy's plan of coming unobserved into the clinic after hours was unravelling faster than a skein of wool in the claws of a cat. It had taken all day to drive from Perth and she'd only arrived half an hour ago. During that time she'd been parked outside in her new car with a cap pulled low on her head so she wouldn't be recognised. She didn't want to talk to anyone in town before she'd seen William and she wanted to read his medical file before she spoke to him.

When Sue had finished her methodical locking-up routine and had double checked everything, Lucy had been certain the clinic was empty and that she was good to go. Even then, she'd held back, checking the immediate area for other cars parked in the clinic car park or nearby. Only then had she been convinced the building was empty.

You got that wrong.

She had to fight hard not to bite her lip. That the man in front of her could grace the runway of a fashion show and make every woman in the crowd swoon was a given, but considering an average-looking guy had just tossed her aside, treating fidelity as if it was completely expendable, she was now giving all men a wide berth. No matter how handsome or how thick, dark and wavy was the hair which fell over the top of tanned ears and teased fingers to brush it back, she would not be tempted. She was especially impervious to square, broad shoulders that despite her being in her highest heels were at perfect head-resting height. She'd been fooled by the promise of a safe haven more than once.

No, the effort required not to bite her lip came from the derisive look that scoured his high cheek bones and burned from his rich-cocoa-coloured eyes. The look that said, I wouldn't touch your hand if you were the last woman on earth.

He crossed his toned arms with their dark hairs almost standing on end over his wide chest and completely ignored her hand. 'I do not know you.' His accent thickened. 'You should not be here.'

You know he's correct.

She gritted her teeth against her conscience and told herself she had the right to be here. Mustering up a smile, the winning one she'd used a lot as a child to get her own way, she forced her hand to stay hovering between them despite wanting to whip it back by her side and dry the sweat on her jeans. All she needed to do was explain who she was and her plan would be safe. 'I'm Lucy Patterson. You emailed me about William.'

'You're William's daughter?' Chocolate brows shot halfway up an intelligent forehead and his gaze raked her from head to toe as disbelief momentarily pushed his anger aside.

She was used to this reaction, having experienced it often from the age of sixteen when it had become obvious she was never going to grow any taller. Once it had made her laugh and she'd had a steady stream of jokes at the ready about her and William's excessive height differences. Only that had been before everything had changed and a lifetime lie had been exposed. 'Like I said, I'm Lucy Patterson.' She tilted her extended hand slightly.

He slowly uncrossed his folded arms and slid his right palm against hers, his long fingers curving around her hand like a splash of dark paint against a white canvas. The heat burned her, shooting up her arm before diving deep and leaving behind a trail of addictive tingles and shivers.

Oh, no. Not now and not here. Shocked at her body's reaction, she abruptly pulled her hand away to the safety of her side. After the debacle that had been her relationship with Daniel, she didn't want or need any type of attraction to any man. Especially one in Bulla Creek where she wouldn't live again even if they paid her.

Marco didn't seem to have noticed her hasty end to their handshake. 'Lucy Patterson, why are you here?'

Lucy wondered if perhaps his English wasn't as good as she'd assumed. She smiled again. 'You wrote to me and asked me to come, so here I am.'

Two deep lines etched into the bridge of his nose. 'I asked you to come and visit your father, not the computer in this office.'

The muscles in her cheeks ached from the continual bright smile. A smile that didn't seem to be having any effect on its intended target. She went for chatty. 'I'm not sure what doctors are like where you come from, but in Australia the combination of being male and a doctor makes the worst type of patient.'

Marco tilted his head in thought and a curl fell forward. 'This may be.'

Yes, she was getting somewhere. 'So it makes sense for me to read his medical history before I see him.'

So now you're lying to other people and not just yourself.

Again, she silenced her conscience. *Let me do things my way.*

Marco continued to stare at her with a questioning look. 'But you are not William's doctor.'

'No, but I *am* a doctor.'

Again his gaze censored her. 'Then you should know better.'

She tossed her head, overriding the sliver of guilt that pierced her and instead converted it into righteous indignation. 'William hasn't mentioned to me that he broke his leg and at his age a fall can be a sign of other things so it makes sense for me to read his file.'

'Your father is not so ill that he can't speak. William is very capable of telling you the information.' A look of realisation suddenly shone brightly in his enigmatic eyes. 'Have you spoken to him?'

She shrugged so as not to squirm and held onto her bravado. 'Thank you for emailing me, but I've got it all under control.' She moved back toward the computer.

In two long strides he was by her side with his hands on her upper arms and suddenly her feet left the floor.

Abject offence roared through her. 'Hey! Put me down.'

A moment later, she was back on terra firma with Marco, feet wide apart, standing solidly between her and the computer and blocking her path.

His glare matched hers—incensed and scowling. 'As William's doctor and partner in this practice, I will not allow you to read his file without his permission.'

She held onto her dignity by a thread. 'I'm his next of kin.'

'*Sí*, so you know that does not give you the right to read his file.' His hand shot out. 'You have a key to the clinic?'

Her arms shot over her chest as guilt and anger hammered her. 'I'm not giving it to you.'

'You do not work here and I do not trust you.'

'I grew up here.' Words spluttered in her throat, chained by a rush of conflicting emotions that made her sway. 'God, I spent so many Saturday mornings playing in the waiting room that it was my second home. You're the stranger here, buddy, not me.'

He didn't even flinch. If anything he seemed more implacable than ever and the quietness of his voice didn't hide for a moment his firm intent. 'Go and talk with your father.'

The prospect of talking to William had anxiety and heartache making her feet twitch in readiness to run far from Bulla Creek. 'I *will* read that file.'

He shook his head. 'Not without William's permission.'

'Fine, I'll ask Sue.'

His jaw stiffened. 'I think that Sue is disappointed that you have not been to see your father in a long time. She will side with me.'

She swallowed hard, hating that the town might have turned on her without knowing the full story. Her hands shot out in bitter aggravation. 'This isn't how we do things in the country.'

This time one brow rose sardonically. 'So, you would let *anyone* read your patients' files where you work? If this is so, I would not want to be under your care.'

The shot against her professionalism jolted her hard.

You know he's right. From before he caught you trying to read the file you've known he was right.

My situation is different. She harnessed all her frustration, using it to push away the other emotions that threatened to swamp her the way they had on and off over the last six months. She fisted her hands by her sides. 'You know nothing about me, Dr Rodriguez, and therefore not enough to judge me.'

Before he could reply, she pushed past him, stalking out into the fading light and back to her car, homeless in a town she'd once called home. Only then did she allow herself to cry.

CHAPTER TWO

'PAPÁ?'

Marco lay on his son's bed as part of their 'goodnight' ritual. 'Yes.'

'No boys…' Ignacio spoke slowly, each word an effort to form perfectly. He breathed in '…have crutches.'

Marco tried to keep the tension out of his voice. 'Lots of boys use crutches.'

'Not at school. Not in town. I looked.'

Marco swallowed a familiar sigh. 'You are right. No other boys in Bulla Creek use crutches, but you're special.'

'No. I'm not.' Ignacio's voice rose and his small body spasmed, making it even more rigid than its usual state. 'I'm different. I don't like it.'

Each word pierced Marco's heart. A part of him knew that one day his wonderful son would make the connection that he didn't have the same free and easy control of his body as most other boys his age. Marco had hoped however that the realisation would come much later than at a mere five years of age. The irony of it all was that inside a body that failed Ignacio daily on so many levels was a mind that was sharp and fiercely intelligent.

'*Querido*, your crutches are your friend when your legs are tired. Now you must sleep so your legs are rested in the morning.'

He slid the soft-toy koala, the one Ignacio had chosen on their arrival at Sydney airport, into his arms and then tucked in the sheet and light blanket around him. Pressing a kiss to his forehead, he whispered, 'I love you. Sleep well.'

'I love you, too, *Papá.*'

Marco closed the door behind him and walked directly to the kitchen. Heather had prepared a plate of cold chicken and salad for him and as he poured himself a glass of wine to accompany the food, he wished he was eating a thick steak straight off the barbecue instead of yet another cold meal. Of course, he could fire up the grill and cook one, but he lacked the energy. Bulla Creek, the place he'd come to as a sanctuary and for a new start, was wearing him out.

As he ate, he glanced at the calendar, mentally calculating how long William had been out of action. It felt disloyal to wish his colleague and mentor back at his desk when he clearly didn't feel up to it and yet if William could give just two hours a day to see the straightforward cases it would ease Marco's load considerably.

Lucy Patterson is a doctor. You could ask her to help.

No. He pushed his plate away and took a long gulp of his wine as the combined image of wild, grey eyes and pale cheeks stained with pink hit him. It was instantly followed up with the backhander of a lush-red, pouting and highly kissable mouth. His blood pounded more than a fraction faster.

He quickly stood up and stowed his plate in the dishwasher as if movement would empty his mind of her. It galled him that his body had decided to come alive in the presence of a woman who looked like a fragile porcelain doll, but in personality was the exact opposite. Plus, she came with questionable professional ethics. A lesser man would have melted under the incensed fire blazing from those eyes, which had flared when he'd denied her access to the computer.

His palms suddenly glowed hot, reliving the soft warmth of her skin where he'd touched her arms. Skin that covered surprisingly taut muscles that had hinted at some weight-work. That he'd lifted her out of the way still shocked him, but he'd acted out of loyalty to William. William was his patient and he knew nothing of Lucy.

William didn't speak of her and Sue had sighed when she'd reluctantly handed over the email address saying, 'He won't be happy about this and she should know better.' At the time, he'd been intent on getting some help for William and by default for himself so Marco hadn't given Sue's statement much thought. However, now he'd met Lucy Patterson, he wondered if it was her conduct as a doctor that was the issue that lay between her and her father. William was one of the most principled and professional doctors Marco had ever worked with and he couldn't imagine him condoning any behaviour that went against his code of practice.

No, it was enough that William would resent his intrusion in summoning his daughter without

Marco adding to it by asking her to work in the clinic. He couldn't in all conscience have someone in the practice who ignored protocol. No, Lucy Patterson wasn't the answer to his problems.

Decision made, he took his wine out onto the back deck which overlooked the surrounding rocky hills and breathed in the sweet, cool evening air that slid in over the fading heat. Out here, he could usually shed some of the pressures that plagued him, but not tonight. As he watched the night star rise in the darkening sky, his thoughts spun out to Argentina and to his parents who were anxious to join him in Bulla Creek the moment he was granted permanent residency and he could legally sponsor them. They missed their grandson. His thoughts bounced back to Ignacio's heartbreak. He let his head fall back on that grief, feeling it moving through him again, just like it had years before, and then suddenly, without any bidding, an image of Lucy Patterson's curvaceous behind swooped in sending all other thoughts scattering.

Swearing in Spanish, he stood up and walked inside.

* * *

Lucy repaired her makeup in the car using the tiny mirror on the visor and then ran a brush through her hair. The yellow light gave her a jaundiced look and she pinched her cheeks trying to infuse some colour. She should have checked into the motel, but she really didn't want to meet anyone she knew until she'd spoken to William. She stared at her pale face. 'Lucy Jane whoever-you-are, it's time.'

Stepping out onto the sweeping, circular drive-way outside Haven, the gravel crunched under her feet and she stared up at the house. The stone and iron cottage with its whitewashed window sills and decorative wooden veranda rails stood as it had for the last one hundred and thirty years. It had been her home from the age of one when her parents had moved with her to Bulla Creek, and right up until she'd left for university. After that it had been her haven when life in Perth pressed in on her, and she'd run home for some rest, relaxation and general cosseting.

All that had changed and now it was a house associated with heartache. Part of her wanted to knock on the front door to emphasise her visitor status, but it was a long walk from the back of the house and no matter how furious she was with William, he would be on crutches. She didn't want him to walk further than necessary so she walked around the side of the house, opened the squeaky gate and entered the cottage garden. The scent of lavender hit her nostrils and she breathed in deeply, trying to use its calming properties. To her left, an enormous grapevine grew over a frame, providing shade to what William had always called 'their outdoor living room'.

Her gaze extended beyond the deck, through the large, glass doors and into the kitchen. She saw William sitting at the long, Baltic pine table, with crutches resting on one end as well as a cane. A book lay in front of him, and he held a glass in his hand. Her heart rolled over despite itself. When had he got old? The last time she'd seen him his hair had had flecks of silver streaking through the black. Now all his hair was silver grey.

Go in, talk to him, and make sure he's okay.

She tossed her head as she grumbled quietly to herself. 'Yes, I'm going inside but after that, I'm checking into the motel.'

Blowing out a breath, she tried to capture a

semblance of composure because everything to do with William always generated a mass of contradictory feelings. She rolled her shoulders back, raised her hand, knocked and walked in.

'Hello, William.'

The man she'd called her father for twenty-six years looked up from his book, shock draining his face of colour. 'Lucy.' He stared at her and blinked, as if he didn't believe his eyes, and then slowly his mouth curved up into a wide and familiar smile. 'What a wonderful surprise.'

She bit her lip, not knowing what to say because 'Just passing through, thought I'd drop in' didn't allow for the seven hundred kilometre journey from Perth. She tilted her head toward the crutches. 'You've been in the wars.'

He raised his leg, the cast white against the dark material of his trousers, and gave a self-deprecating grimace. 'Came off my bike dodging a kangaroo. Big red hopped away and now I'm hopping too.'

His humour circled her like it always had—warm and loving—but she refused to give in to it because being a doctor was so much easier than the minefield of being his daughter. 'So I see. Any other damage besides a fractured tibia?'

His smile faded slightly. 'How do you know I have a fractured tibia? I haven't mentioned what bones I broke.'

Busted. But she had no qualms telling him the truth because she had no need to protect the source, especially given what had happened. 'Your Spanish doctor emailed me.'

For some reason her face felt suddenly hot, which was crazy because she hadn't even said the man's name. However, since she'd stormed out of the clinic, each time she'd thought about the raven-haired, accented doctor, this heat-fest flared inside her. She wanted it to stop.

'He's not Spanish. He's from Argentina.' William's face sagged, making him look more haggard than ever. 'So, the *only* reason you're in Bulla Creek is because Marco asked you to come?'

She shrugged trying not to let his palpable hurt touch her. She was hurting too, only her reason was much bigger and more life-altering than his. 'I'm here to make sure you're getting the right medical care.'

This time William shrugged and when he spoke his voice held the well-modulated tone of a country GP giving a report to a colleague. 'You can set your mind at ease immediately. Marco is more than competent and the break wasn't complicated, but even so he insisted on me going to Geraldton to see Jeremy Lucas, the orthopod. As you can see, I'm doing well and I've graduated to a walking stick.'

She wanted to believe him, but evidence to the contrary was in front of them. 'So why the crutches?'

'I was tired tonight after more walking more than usual so I've been using crutches. If you don't believe me about the break, you can look at the X-rays if you wish.'

'Dr Rodriguez wouldn't let me look at anything.'

He frowned again. 'You've been to the clinic?'

She shifted on her feet realising there was absolutely nothing wrong with her father's lightning-quick brain. It was a good thing except when it pertained to her. 'I had to drive past the clinic to get here so it made sense to call in first.'

You're big on self-delusion today.

She kept talking to silence her conscience. 'But like I said, he wouldn't give me any information and he told me in no uncertain terms...' she found herself gently stroking the tops of her arms and dropped her hands away fast '...that I had to talk to you.'

'As it should be.' His lips twitched. 'Still, I imagine that would have been very frustrating for you.' The words held the type of understanding that only came from knowing someone for a very long time, and they held a slight hint of censure.

'It was.' She braced herself, expecting him to say something about the fact she hadn't spoken to him in months.

He cleared his throat. 'As you can see I'm doing fine and the cast comes off in a few days. Sharon comes in each day to cook and clean just as she has all year, and Sue calls in as well. There's absolutely nothing for you to worry about.'

William rose to his feet and ignoring the crutches used his cane to rest against. 'Cup of tea?'

She hesitated, rationalising that he sounded

fine and he seemed to have everything organised without her help so she didn't have to stay.

He doesn't look fine. He looks tired, old and sad.

She didn't want to think about that because it tempted her to question the decision she'd made months ago. 'Um…thanks, but it's been a long day and…um…I still need to check into the motel.'

'The motel?' William's movement stalled and his face paled. 'Lucy, you know you *always* have a room here if you want or need it.' He stared at her silently, not asking her to stay in words but with his hazel eyes which filled with quiet hope.

She swallowed, trying to hold herself together as the long drive, her horrible last two days and the fracas in the clinic slammed into the comforting scent of bergamot, fresh mint and leather-bound books—some of the many fragrances that defined her childhood. Despite the catastrophic disclosure that had changed everything, despite her anger and confusion regarding William and Bulla Creek, the aromas of yesteryear pulled at her strongly, upending her plan of a quick, clinical visit.

Fatigue clawed at her like sticky mud on boots and the thought of having to deal with the questioning looks of Loretta, the gossipy motel owner, was more than she could bear. She was a grown-up, not a child, and surely she could get through *one* night in this house with all its ghosts. One night of duty to really make sure William was doing as well as he said.

She sank into the comforting depths of the chesterfield before she could talk herself out of it and said, 'Tea would be lovely, thank you.'

Lucy squinted against the bright sunlight which poured into her bedroom through the now thin and faded pink curtains. She flipped onto her side, pulling the pillow over her head, but then the raucous screech of the white cockatoos greeting the dawn shocked her fully awake. As her heart rate slowed, she remembered she was lying in her childhood bed in Haven, back at Bulla Creek.

This time her heart rate stayed normal, but her stomach squirted acid. At this rate, her stress levels were going to seriously injure her. She threw back the covers. Shower first and then food.

Twenty minutes later she padded into the kitchen, totally starving and on the search for breakfast.

She found a note on the pantry door scrawled in William's trademark black ink and squinted, trying to decipher it. No nib, however fine, had ever improved his doctor's handwriting. Seeing it drew her back in time to when she'd been a fourteen-year-old girl watching the man she hero-worshipped writing at the old oak desk in the study and telling her that the fountain pen, which had been his father's, would belong to her one day.

Just think, Lucy, there could be three generations of doctors in the family writing prescriptions with the same pen. Wouldn't that be special?

At the time she'd thought it would be amazingly special because it meant the need to care and heal ran so strongly in the Pattersons' veins it couldn't be denied, and she was part of that destiny.

Lucy gave herself a shake and centred her thoughts on the prosaic present. William no longer wrote prescriptions with the fountain pen because they were computer generated and printed, and she wasn't certain the pen represented anything any more other than being part of the elaborate fake facade of her life.

She read the note.

I hope you'll stay for lunch. My treat at the Shearer's Arms at noon? Either way, please don't go without a goodbye. Dad x

Last time she'd left Haven she'd run through a veil of tears propelled by anger and the devastating cost of a lifelong lie. Ironically, she was back here not only to check up on William, but because of another lie. Only the loss of Daniel didn't hurt anywhere near as much as the loss of Jess.

She ran her hands through her hair, missing her friend who she'd always turned to for advice, especially after the death of Ruth when everything had gone so pear-shaped. Now she had no one to talk to.

I give good advice. Not that you listen much.

She ignored her own unsolicited advice and glanced at the huge station-style clock in the kitchen, its black hands showing that it wasn't even seven. Five long hours until lunch.

Facing William alone over lunch.

She knew he would have booked the alcove

table, the one tucked away from prying eyes and flapping ears so they could 'talk'. She pressed her temples with her fingers. She didn't want to do that, but then again she really didn't want to leave abruptly again either. Putting the invitation into the 'too hard basket', she filled the kettle and set it to boil before opening the pantry door. She stepped inside its cool walls. The usually groaning shelves were under-stocked and as she reached for a box of breakfast cereal, her gaze landed on a blister pack of tablets that were slid in next to the breakfast condiments. She picked them up, turned them over and read the name. *Anti-hypertensive tablets*. She frowned. How long had William been taking blood pressure medication?

The doctor in her wanted to ask him right now, but waking him up to do that wasn't the best idea. She picked up the cereal and noticed the box was almost empty. She checked the fridge, which had no yoghurt and only a small amount of milk. She pulled open the freezer and apart from a sports pack and a bag of peas and one casserole, it was predominantly filled with ice. Grabbing a pen, she wrote a shopping list, and then she pulled six grocery bags from the pantry and picked up her keys. Before she left Bulla Creek, she'd make sure William had a full pantry and a few more frozen meals.

The supermarket manager was just opening the doors when Lucy arrived in town. She didn't know him, but she gave him a nod as she passed through and wrestled with a trolley which didn't want to leave its pack. Welcoming the chance to focus on groceries, which were delightfully simple compared with everything else in her life, she started collecting the ingredients for a variety of casseroles. The radio blared loudly and she sang along with the music right up to when she presented her load to the checkout. She'd just started placing her items on the black conveyer belt when she jumped at the blast of an air horn and dropped a can of tomatoes.

'Loud, eh?' The heavily made-up teenager grinned. 'That's Jason saying "G'day". He always does that when he's taking a load of sheep to Perth. He does it when he comes back too so Kylie knows he's safe.'

'And no one's ever asked him not to?' Lucy's

adrenaline surge was fading, leaving her jittery and slightly on edge.

The girl looked at her as if she had two heads. 'No. You get used to it when you—'

The gut-wrenching sound of the long screech of rubber against asphalt deafened all other noise, followed immediately by the chilling crunch of metal against metal.

Lucy ran. As her feet hit the pavement she looked left, but could only see heat haze shimmering on the road. Then she looked right and gagged. A jack-knifed truck lay on its side along with a four-deck trailer full of sheep. Sheep were everywhere—some standing, some bloodied and bleeding, but Lucy's eyes passed over them as she saw the driver climbing out of the cabin. She ran to her car, picked up her medical bag and kept running.

When she reached the driver, he was walking in circles, his hands pulling at his hair and blood pouring down his face. 'Jason? You need to sit down.' Lucy took his arm and shepherded him toward the kerb, wanting to check his pupils for a concussion.

His unfocused gaze settled on her face. 'She came from nowhere.'

Lucy didn't know what he meant. 'Who's she?'

'The other car.'

The other car? She spun around, her eyes searching beyond the truck and the bleating sheep.

'Lucy!' Deb, an off-duty nurse from the hospital, ran up to her breathless. 'Geraldine Carter's in the other car.'

Oh, God, she couldn't even see another car and a thousand thoughts ran through her head. 'Get Dr Rodriguez, ring the police, find someone to stay with Jason and then come and help me.'

As she ran, she heard the scream of sirens in the distance and gave thanks, knowing the police and local volunteer fire brigade would block off the road and sort out the sheep. She rounded the truck and braced herself for what she imagined would be horrific.

She breathed in hard to keep from retching.

What had once been a small hatch-back car was now smashed almost beyond recognition. The impact of the crash had flattened the passenger side of the car before pushing it off the road into the low stone fence of the community park. A woman was slumped forward over the steering wheel, deathly still.

Checking there were no power lines touching the car, Lucy gripped the car door handle and prayed it would open without needing the cutting skill of the 'jaws of life'. She gave an almighty pull and felt some give so tugged again. Grudgingly, the door opened just enough for her to squeeze in. She put her hand on the woman's shoulder. 'Can you hear me?'

The woman didn't move. What had Deb said her name was? 'Geraldine, can you hear me?' She heard a moan. 'I'm Lucy and a doctor and I'm going to help you.'

Airway, breathing, circulation. Lucy pressed her fingers against the woman's neck, feeling for the carotid pulse. *Thready.* Carefully, using her hands as a brace, she brought Geraldine's head into a neutral line. She needed to apply a cervical collar, but to do that she needed to sit her upright. Ideally, it was a two-person job.

Hurry up, Marco.

Airway comes first. She knew she didn't have time to wait, especially when she had no clue how far away help was from arriving. 'Geraldine, I'm going to move—'

'What's her condition?'

Thank you. Lucy had never been so pleased to hear a Spanish accent in her life and she swivelled her head around in relief. Intelligent, dark brown eyes filled with a host of medical questions gazed at her, backlit with care and concern.

A odd, fleeting half-thought amidst the chaos of the moment made her wonder how it might feel to be the focus of that sort of caring.

She brushed it aside as completely irrelevant. 'She's conscious, although only just, and given her pulse rate, probably bleeding somewhere. We need to treat her as a possible spinal injury.'

Marco nodded and tugged on the door which shifted, giving them a bit more room, but they'd need a lot more to get Geraldine out of the car. He turned and yelled to the police sergeant, 'Graham, we need this door off.'

'On it.'

Lucy heard Graham on his two-way radio to the fire brigade and then Marco moved in next to her, filling the cramped space with his clean, fresh citrus scent and the welcome support of professional reinforcement. 'Geraldine, this is Marco. We're going to carefully sit you up and protect your neck.'

The woman groaned without forming any words.

Lucy continued in triage mode. 'Marco, you support her mid-thorax and I'll support her neck. On my count. One, two, three.'

They sat Geraldine up and then without being asked, Marco passed Lucy the cervical collar.

'This will support your neck, Geraldine.' She quickly wrapped it into position.

'Lucy, take this.'

She turned and Marco held out the equipment she needed to attach Geraldine to the Propaq so they could monitor her vital signs. 'Thanks.'

He nodded. 'I'll insert the IV.'

'Sorry, Geraldine, but I have to rip your shirt.' The woman's eyes flickered open and shut again. Lucy tugged at the buttons on the blouse and they came open and she applied the patches to the woman's skin. A moment later, the machine beeped into life. 'BP's low. Two lines would be good.'

'Oxygen too.' He shoved the green mask and

plastic tubing into her hands and then he returned to his task, his forehead scored deep with worry lines. He quietly reassured a barely conscious Geraldine while his fingers moved up and down her arm seeking a viable vein. He tightened the tourniquet and tried again.

Lucy wanted to watch, wanted to will a vein to appear but she knew it wouldn't help. Her job was to check Geraldine's pupils' reaction to light and hopefully rule out a head injury. They each did their job, working as a team and pooling their body of knowledge as they scrambled to stabilise their patient. They spoke few words, but the ones they voiced locked together to build a synchronicity that flowed between them.

'IV is in.'

'Great. Push fluids.'

Marco pumped in a litre of Hartmann's through the hard-won IV line in a furious attempt to bring up Geraldine's blood pressure.

Blocking out the bleating of sheep and all other extraneous noises, Lucy moved her stethoscope around Geraldine's chest. The woman was taking short, shallow breaths and her pulse-ox numbers stayed low despite the help of the oxygen. 'I think she's got a tension pneumothorax.'

Marco's frown deepened. He handed the bag of Hartmann's to a bystander saying, 'Hold it high.'

The young man nodded and did as he was asked while Marco passed gloves, antiseptic and a large bore needle to Lucy. 'Needle decompression.'

Lucy snapped on the gloves and sloshed the brown antiseptic onto Geraldine's skin. 'Second intercostal space at the level of the angle of Louis.'

'*Sí*. Then gentle traction on the plunger and checking for air bubbles.'

Lucy knew it all, but saying it out loud to a colleague and hearing confirmation always helped. 'And then an immediate relief of symptoms.'

I hope. Her fingers located the position and she pressed the needle into place, praying the needle wouldn't block. The beeping of the monitor faded.

'*Beuno*, you're in. Pulse-ox is rising now.' The relief in Marco's deep voice vibrated around them, matching her own. 'Leave the needle open.'

'Yep, had planned to.' The rush of a good save flowed through her. Although Geraldine wasn't out of the woods yet, at least they'd sorted out one big problem.

The sensation lasted ninety seconds.

The sharp and incessant beeping of the Propaq rose again, screaming at them as their patient's heart rate soared and her blood pressure plummeted. For the briefest moment, Marco's gaze met hers and she had an overwhelming moment of connection, unlike anything she'd ever experienced with a colleague.

Their words collided as they both yelled out in unison, 'Jaws of life now!'

CHAPTER THREE

THE emergency helicopter banked and quickly headed south towards Perth, taking the deafening noise of the rotors with it, and exposing the continual bleating of injured and scared sheep. Marco ran his hand through his hair and glanced at Lucy. They'd worked side by side for over an hour and he still had the alluring scent of her perfume in his nostrils. Call him overtired, but he'd swear it was a combination of vanilla and liquorice. At first he'd breathed in deeply, using the scent as a shield when the smell of blood and fear had threatened to choke him. After that, he'd just wanted her scent—wanted it badly, like a smoker needed his next cigarette.

Lucy was staring down at her feet and her smooth and sleek hair fell forward across her cheeks like a curtain, masking her face and masking her emotions. Not that it mattered—even when he could see her expressions, he couldn't work her out. Today, she'd been a totally different person from yesterday, running the emergency expertly and efficiently, and without any of the high drama and emotion that had been on display in the practice. She knew her medicine and he'd been grudgingly impressed. Given the difficult conditions, they'd worked together well, anticipating each other's needs as if they'd worked together for years. All he had to do now was think of her in terms of a doctor rather than a woman and his life could return to normal. How hard could that be?

As if she could sense his gaze on her, she raised her head, tucked her hair behind her ears and attempted a smile, only the accompanying tension thwarted it. 'It's going to be touch and go, isn't it?'

He nodded, sharing the exact same concerns for Geraldine. 'It is, but together we've given her a chance. Thank goodness the accident happened in the town because otherwise...'

'Yeah.' She nodded. 'She'd be dead like so many of these poor sheep.'

A team of farmers had arrived to tend to the injured sheep and a shot fired out, the first of many.

Lucy flinched before giving a self-deprecating laugh. 'Obviously I've been living the city-girl life for too long.'

He smiled wryly. 'No one likes to see animals injured. Even the farmers are going to find this tough.'

'True.' She tilted her head as if she was sending some sort of non-verbal message to him.

He turned and saw small groups of people gathering, all edging towards them looking slightly stunned and shocked, and needing to talk about what had happened so they could absorb it and put it into perspective. His day, already late starting due to the emergency, just got even busier.

You've got a competent doctor standing in front of you so use her.

The thought of how he'd warned her off yesterday loomed large in his mind, but he could no longer deny the fact that he was exhausted and with this disaster he absolutely needed help.

'Lucy.' The rest of the sentence stuck in his throat.

'Yes?' She shoved her hands into the pockets of her cargo pants and rocked back and forth on the balls of her feet as if she wanted to move away and move fast.

He swallowed and forced up the words. 'Can you examine the driver of the truck for me, please, while I get started on the day's work?'

Her chestnut brows rose to her hairline. 'Are you sure you trust me in the clinic?'

He sighed, knowing he should have seen that coming. 'Based on how you treated Geraldine, I trust your clinical skills implicitly. I appeal to your conscience and ethical standards that you respect the rules regarding confidentiality, and unless you have William's written permission, you do not look at his file.'

He held his breath, half expecting her to hit him with an Australian expression that said he could damn well work on his own.

Her grey eyes flickered. 'Fair enough.'

He blinked. 'Excuse me?'

It was her turn to sigh. 'Yesterday…' She tugged at her bottom lip with her teeth.

Mesmerised, his gaze dropped, glued to her plump mouth and the flash of white against ruby-red. Heat socked him, rushing into every crevice and he instantly wondered if the visual lushness they promised would be matched by the touch of his lips against hers.

Now isn't the best time for this.

Horrified that he was lusting after a colleague—especially after he'd just given a speech on professionalism—he dragged his eyes to her face and tried to remember what they were talking about. 'You were saying?'

She cleared her throat. 'Yesterday, I was a little bit...strung out. I haven't seen William in a long time and...'

He thought about his ex-wife, about his parents and siblings and had a moment of understanding. 'Family can make you crazy sometimes.'

'You have no idea.' She lifted her chin sharply in an increasingly familiar action and her hair fell back from her cheeks. 'As much as I hate to admit it, yesterday you had a point.'

He couldn't stop the triumphant smile racing across his face. 'So, you are saying I was right?'

She crossed her arms, but a twitch of her lips softened the rebellious stance and her voice held a teasing air. 'I could agree with you or I could help you out. You choose.'

An unexpected sense of lightness streaked in

under the stress of the last hour, which was layered on top of the permanent tension of his life and his fears for Ignacio. He grinned, enjoying the banter and the fact that she'd made him laugh. His days were divided into being a doctor and being a father, but right now, in this moment he was Marco and that didn't happen very often. 'For now, I will take your help.'

'Done.' Lucy shielded her eyes and squinted up the street. 'Looks like Deb's got the driver in the ambulance so I'll go with them to the hospital.' With a quick wave she walked away, dodging stray sheep.

He should have turned and headed towards his car, but he stood watching the seductive swing of her hips and the way the material of her pants caressed the sweet curve of her behind. His fingers flexed into the same shape and his blood descended with a rush to his groin.

'Marco. Dr Rodriguez?'

Through a fog of lust, he somehow recognised his name and he jerked his head around so hard that he heard a crunch. Emily Blair, a young mother from the primary school, stood staring at him with a slight frown on her face and a disposable coffee cup in her hand. She'd been very kind to him and Ignacio since their arrival, often bringing around food and inviting Ignacio on play dates. Marco knew Emily wanted more out of their friendship, but he didn't want to offer her more. He didn't want to offer any woman more because it was easier that way. No one got hurt.

'Are you okay, Marco? You look a bit...'

Aroused. Turned on. Marco uttered a silent oath and tried to think cold and chilling thoughts. What was it about Lucy Patterson that had him acting like a teenage boy? He mentally started listing off all the bones in the body until his blood returned to his brain and common sense resumed.

Emily pushed the coffee toward him. 'You don't look your normal self, but it was a pretty horrible accident. I thought you might need some coffee.'

'*Gracias.* This is very thoughtful of you.' He accepted the cup being careful not to brush her hand with his.

'Do you need to talk about it?'

Her hopeful expression made him feel like a jerk. 'I am sorry, but I cannot stay and talk. I need to get back to the clinic because I have patients waiting.' He started to back away and raised the coffee in a salute. 'Thank you again, Emily.'

He turned before he saw disappointment line her face.

Three hours later, Marco couldn't quite believe that he was standing in an empty waiting room. He leaned against the counter and spoke to Lisa, the clinic's friendly receptionist. 'I thought there must be something wrong with the computer. There must be more people to see me, no?'

Lisa shook her head with a smile. 'Not until afternoon clinic starts at two. Don't look so worried. For once you get a lunch break.'

Yet, based on his patient load over the last few weeks, none of this made sense. 'But I started late and—'

'Didn't Sue tell you?'

'Tell me what?'

'Lucy Patterson's been seeing patients all morning.'

As if on cue, he heard Lucy's musical voice drifting down the corridor saying, 'Make an appointment with Dr Rodriguez for Friday and by then your blood test results will be back. Meanwhile, David, the most important thing for you is to get some rest.'

A moment later David Saunders appeared at the desk and Marco turned, walking directly to William's consulting room. Lucy was reaching over the examination table, stripping it of linen and his gaze immediately zeroed in on her bottom. 'You—' His voice cracked and he cleared his throat. 'You stayed?'

She straightened up, tossing the sheet into the skip. 'I did.' She flicked out a clean sheet and shot him a smile. 'I had to hang around for Jason's head injury checks so I had the choice of catching up on all the celebrity gossip from last year's magazines or helping you out with your morning list. Didn't Sue tell you?'

Her smile was doing odd things to his breathing and his pulse. He swallowed before managing to say, 'No.'

A single line appeared between her brows. 'Was it the wrong thing to do? I thought you wanted my help?'

He realised between his confusion at learning she was still here and his body's lust-fest with her cute behind, he was frowning at her. He made himself smile. '*Sí*, I did want your help for the truck driver, but I did not expect you to do more. Thank you. It was very generous of you to stay.'

She shrugged as she smoothed down the paper-protector over the sheet. 'Not really.'

This woman was a mass of contradictions and just like yesterday evening, he was immediately back to not understanding her. 'But you came to Bulla Creek to spend your time with William, not to work here.'

She briskly tucked her hair behind her ear, the action defensive. '*Really*, it's not a problem. I was happy to help.'

And he was very appreciative of it. Appreciative of her. Remembering Lisa's words about a real lunch break, he said, 'Can I buy you lunch to thank you?'

'Oh, God, lunch.' Her pupils dilated so wide they almost obliterated the grey, and her hand flew to her mouth as if he'd just suggested something completely inappropriate.

Hell, had she noticed him staring at her behind? *No, she had her back to you.*

He ran his hand through his hair, wondering if being off the dating scene for seven years and only having one night stands had affected his judgement. 'Inviting you to lunch, this was the wrong thing to say?'

'No. It was totally the right thing to say.' She picked up her bag, grabbed his arm, and started pulling him toward the door. 'I'm starving. Let's eat right now.'

The delicious warmth of her hand seeped into him and immediately combined with her enthralling scent. He knew he should resist the tug of that intoxicating pleasure which pooled inside him and that he should press his feet to the floor and refuse to follow her. He knew without a doubt he should pause and question her on why one minute she was horrified by a simple lunch invitation and the next minute she was crazily overenthusiastic.

Knowing and doing were two separate things and he ignored common sense, letting the river of desire that burned in him rule. He allowed himself be led out of the clinic and marched up the street like a teenage boy in lust for the very first time.

The Shearer's Arms was the oldest building in town, pre-dating the church by a good ten years.

A large, rectangular, whitewashed building, it stood at the top end of Main Street with its distinctive red corrugated-iron veranda. Large tables sat under its shade and the regulars could sit and catch the passing breeze while keeping their eye on the activities of the town.

By the time they reached the door, Marco had regained his composure and was determined to reclaim control as the host of the lunch. As he reached for the door handle ahead of Lucy so he could usher her inside, she stopped abruptly and stood staring at the door. 'Are you okay?' She looked as if her thoughts were miles away and she didn't respond. 'Lucy?'

A slight tremor flicked across her shoulders and she gave him a brittle smile. 'Let's go in, shall we?'

He tilted his head and smiled. 'That was my plan.'

He'd expected a laugh, but if anything she seemed even tenser as she ducked under his arm and walked straight past the sign that said, 'Please wait to be seated.'

This wasn't going quite as he'd planned. 'Lucy.'

She didn't slow or turn.

'Dr Patterson.'

Not even the use of her professional name made her pause. Irritation rolled through him like the prickle of a burr. Silently rebuking himself on letting his body overrule his brain, and regretting having issued the lunch invitation, he reluctantly followed her to the furthest corner of the dining room, feeling like a consort trailing behind a queen.

She disappeared behind a partition and he heard her say, 'Sorry we're late.'

Late? He rounded the faux-wood panel and came face to face with William.

The elder doctor leaned against his stick and for the briefest moment confusion flitted across his face, followed by regret. Both were instantly replaced by a polite smile, which looked like it needed the muscles to haul really hard to raise the corners of his mouth. He extended his hand and in a voice that was neither friendly nor unfriendly said, 'Marco.'

'William.' He gripped the GP's hand for the first time since he'd emailed Lucy without William's permission.

'What a pleasant surprise.' William finished the firm handshake and dropped his arm by his side.

Marco was left with the overwhelming sensation that not only was William displeased with his interference, he wasn't happy that Marco was standing at his lunch table. 'I don't want to impose.'

'You're not.' Lucy's hand wrapped itself around his forearm again, but this time with a grip stronger than super-glue. 'Is he, William?'

The pressure of her fingers dug in toward the bone. Marco caught the unambiguous challenge in her eyes as she fixed her stare on her father and he heard its match in her voice. His gaze flicked between father and daughter, not understanding at all and wondering what was going on. Why was Lucy addressing her father by his first name?

'It's not an imposition, Marco.' The well-mannered William didn't skip a beat. 'Have a seat and I'll ask Felicity to set an extra place.'

'The steak here's always good, isn't it, William?' Lucy's hand stayed in place on his arm as she sat down, almost dragging Marco with her.

William hung his walking stick on the edge of

the table with a sad smile. 'I'm glad you remember that.'

With a trembling hand, Lucy picked up a glass of water and lifted it to her mouth, downing it in one, large gulp.

What is going on? Torn between wanting to do the right thing by William but at the same time experiencing an unexpected need to protect Lucy, Marco reluctantly sat down next to her. Suffocating tension hung over the table encasing the Pattersons and by default, oozing out to include him. It completely blocked any feelings of relaxation that should have come from his first real lunch break in weeks. The irony of it all hit hard. Bringing Lucy back to Bulla Creek to help cheer up William might not be the quick fix he was hoping for.

Lucy's skin tingled as she felt Marco's questioning gaze on her, but she kept her head down as if the pattern on the placemat was the most fascinating thing she'd ever seen. Hot and cold chills zipped through her— heat from the touch of those inky eyes and cold from the fact she'd shanghaied him into lunch to use him as a brick wall to William's anticipated lunch for two. Although, given that a different person from the restaurant or bar was walking over to the table every couple of minutes to ask if they had an update on Geraldine and to thank them for their efforts earlier in the day, she probably needn't have dragged him here.

In between interruptions, they gave their orders to the waitress but even the arrival of the food didn't stop the townsfolk. As they ate, they answered questions and finally everyone drifted away. The uncomfortable silence shot back into place.

'It was fortunate Lucy was in town this morning.' Marcos's lilting accent elongated the syllables of each word. 'It would have been very hard on my own.'

'It was fortunate.' William ran his index finger around the edge of a coaster.

Lucy flicked a quick look at Marco to see if he'd detected the soft accusation in William's voice that she'd left Haven before he'd got up, just as he'd expected her to. This time it was Marco who had his head down. She noticed his hair fell over his collar and kicked up around his ears in a mass of curls. On most people it would have screamed, overdue for a haircut, but with Marco it seemed to fit. An image of a gaucho—the famous Argentine cowboys of the pampas—flitted into her mind and she immediately imagined him well seated on a horse, galloping across the grasslands with the wind tearing through his hair.

A flush of heat started at her toes and finished at her scalp. The urge to pant was strong and she gulped more water.

William continued, 'Why were you up and out so early?'

'To stock up your pantry.' She refilled her glass and changed the topic. The only way she could deal with William was to put some professional distance between them and be a doctor. 'Given Geraldine's injuries, I suspect she'll be in an induced coma for at least twenty-four hours and possibly longer. It's odd to think that if I hadn't have been in Bulla Creek treating her, she'd probably have been my patient at Perth City.'

'In Emergency, the operating theatre or ICU?' Marco put his knife and fork together on his now-empty plate and smiled at the waitress who quickly removed it.

His smile fascinated Lucy. It started with a lop-sided grin before evening out with both sides of his wide and full mouth pulled up into a broad curve. That action set up dimples twirling into his cheeks before the smile spun out into deep crinkles around darkly delicious and enigmatic eyes.

The traitorous warmth stirred inside her again.

'Lucy's currently torn between Surgery and Emergency.'

William's voice shocked her attention back to the fact she hadn't answered Marco's question and her cheeks burned.

Stop gazing at him. Focus. Remember Daniel and what he did to you?

She immediately justified her actions as window-shopping. After all, where was the harm in that?

Smoothing her napkin against her lap, she looked directly at William. 'Actually, I've just applied for a third year position in Emergency, but I'm thinking of pulling it and applying for a similar job in London.'

William's sharp intake of breath and subsequent cough had Marco quickly refilling his water glass. 'Are you all right?'

William nodded and took a drink. 'Fine. Never better.'

Marco didn't look convinced.

The waitress arrived with coffee orders and three large slabs of chocolate cake. William thanked her and picked up his cake fork. 'Marco, given that you weren't very happy with Lucy yesterday, and justifiably so, how did you find working with my daughter today?'

This time Marco spluttered and shot her a look that traded entrapment with stunned surprise. She returned it, having never heard William— who was known for his mildness—to be quite so direct.

She answered for Marco, feeling slightly guilty she'd put him in this position and because she'd been out of line the day before. 'He told me he doesn't have any problems with my clinical skills.'

William ignored her. 'Marco?'

A faint line creased his brow and he took a moment to reply. 'Lucy knows her emergency medicine. I didn't see her with any other patients so I cannot comment on that.'

'Excuse me,' her voice rose, 'but this is lunch, not an assessment of me. I helped out today, end of story.' She shovelled a huge piece of cake onto her fork, needing the sugar hit.

'Actually, it *is* an assessment of you. I need to know if Marco would be happy to have you work in the practice until I'm back on my feet.'

Her cake-laden fork clattered to the plate. 'Shouldn't the first question be to me, asking if *I'm* happy to work in the practice?'

William shook his head and spoke quietly. 'No. Marco is a practice partner and you're not.'

Practice partner. It was like an open-handed hit to the face and a torrent of emotions flooded her, confusing her even more. Anger quickly dominated over heartache. 'I have a job, Da—William. In Perth, remember.'

'I'm fully aware of that, Lucy.' His voice was quiet but firm. 'However, until recently you always said you wanted to work here.'

She wanted to yell, *That was before everything changed*, but she stopped herself in time. She wasn't about to share private information with Marco that belonged between herself and William. Furious with him, she said, 'Marco has concerns about me and patient confidentiality.'

'Marco contacted you without my permission so you're both as bad as each other. However I'm taking it as a compliment that you both care about me.' A determined glint lit up William's hazel eyes. 'Lucy, this is your chance to see if your decision to give up on taking over the Bulla Creek practice was the right one.'

The double meaning—'giving up on me'—wasn't lost on her, and she felt herself being backed fast into a corner. As she started to formulate a reply—one that couldn't be argued away—Marco joined in with, 'Your father's cast is off in three days. I'm sure you planned to visit for at least this long, yes?'

Her chest tightened. Oh, God. If she said 'No' she looked like the daughter from hell and despite everything that had happened she didn't want that tag, especially as she really hadn't done anything to earn it. She glanced at William, stunned by his strong-arm tactics which she'd never seen before, and then she looked back at Marco.

His tanned face showed signs of deeply entrenched fatigue and the quiet sort of desperation that stemmed from that. 'I could use your help.'

She didn't owe Marco anything and she tried to resist the pull of his words. Hell, she'd only just met the man, but she knew enough about men to know they hated asking for help. The fact he had meant he must really need it and it prompted the question of why. But helping Marco meant complying with William's request and the fall-out from that was staying at Haven. Sharing the house with William.

'It's only three days.'

William's well-modulated Australian accent melded with Marco's Spanish one, circling her, entreating her, but with two very different reasons.

Feeling trapped, she bit her lip. *Three days.* She wasn't thrilled about the idea at all and yet, she supposed if she was honest with herself, she'd always known she'd probably have to spend at least two days in Bulla Creek anyway. Work would keep her busy, making the time pass quickly.

You'll be working with eye-candy, Marco.

She gritted her teeth and reminded herself that she was only window-shopping. Subverting her treacherous body's adolescent rips of desire wouldn't be hard. Hell, she'd only just broken up with Daniel so no way was she ready to jump feet first into a new relationship. Given the mess her life was currently in, that would be the icing on a cake of insanity. No, the hard part would be staying with William, but given the emergency this morning, she hadn't even completed her plan of filling his freezer or asking him about the medication in the pantry. She might not consider herself his daughter any more, but the doctor in her wouldn't let her walk away until she was certain he was as well as he could be.

Determined not to appear to be a woman easily manipulated or a push-over, she tossed her head and jutted her chin. 'Three days, but that's all.'

The two men at the table smiled.

CHAPTER FOUR

SWEAT poured off Lucy as she stood inside a tin shack thirty kilometres out of Bulla Creek trying to convince Iva Labowski that he needed to come into town and spend a night in one of the hospital beds. It was the absolute opposite of the state-of-the-art hospital she worked at in Perth, but then again she didn't do home visits in Perth.

She'd deliberately left this visit until last, because according to a tight-lipped Sue at the morning practice meeting, the old Polish prospector wouldn't be happy about leaving. The practice nurse had been correct.

Lucy gambled on medical grounds. 'Your blood sugar's too high and the ulcer on your leg's looking nasty.'

Iva wore a mulish expression. 'Send the nurse.'

'She's the one who sent me.' Lucy tried appealing to the old bachelor through his stomach.

'Just think, you won't have to cook for a couple of nights.'

'I cook good food here.'

Lucy attempted not to recoil at the sight of the fly-infested food which sat uncovered on the sagging bench. 'I'm sure you do, but Rachel cooks the best roast lamb in the district, not to mention her crispy golden roast potatoes.'

He reached down and fondled the ears of his aging red cattle dog. 'I no leave Rusty.'

Lucy mopped the back of her neck with an alcohol-impregnated wipe and wondered how Iva had survived fifty summers in this shack, when she was melting on a balmy spring day of only thirty-three degrees Celsius outside. She was worried about his leg and the ever-increasing risk of gangrene. She sighed, feeling defeated. 'Rusty can stay with me.'

Iva's rheumy eyes narrowed as if he was looking at her for the first time and in his heavy accent said, 'You like your mother.'

The words stabbed into Lucy's heart like a blunt knife and she swallowed against a wave of pain. 'I don't look anything like Ruth.'

He shook his head and put a gnarly hand on his

heart. 'She look after Rusty when I go to Perth for heart operation. You right. You no look like her, but you have her heart.'

I don't. Lucy didn't want to talk about the woman she'd loved and trusted. 'So it's settled. You're both coming to Bulla Creek. Let's pack a bag.'

'I think I'm in love with air-conditioning,' Lucy said two hours later as she filled out the blood slip before handing it to Deb, the hospital duty nurse.

'I know what you mean. I'm getting more love at the moment from technology than I am from any man,' Deb quipped as she selected the appropriate blood tubes.

Lucy laughed. 'And all you need are rechargeable batteries. Still, with the ratio of men to women in Bulla Creek, technically you should be fighting them off with a stick.'

'True, but it's the ones you want that are always the ones you can't have.'

'Ohh, now I'm intrigued. Who doesn't want to be got?'

Deb picked up the kidney dish with all the venipuncture equipment. 'I need to take Iva's blood.'

'Remember, I know just about everyone in town,' Lucy teased, 'so I'll work it out eventually.'

'Hello.' Marco walked up to the desk with a polite smile that included both of them, but his gaze quickly slid away from Lucy until it was entirely focused on the nurse. 'Debra, I am changing Mrs Luxton's medication. Please can you give her the first dose of the antibiotics now?'

Two bright pink dots stained Deb's cheeks. 'Sure thing, Marco.'

'*Gracias.* Flucloxacillan. I wrote it on the chart.'

Lucy watched Deb hurry off.

So bachelor Marco's the man who doesn't want to be got. Good thing I don't want him then.

Her skin suddenly tingled and she swung around to see Marco's dark chocolate eyes watching her with a burning intensity that sucked the breath from her lungs. Her heart tripped and a ribbon of unexpected longing tore through her making her legs weak. She was thankful she was still sitting down.

Marco blinked and a second later he was looking at her the way he always did—with no interest in her other than as a colleague.

Her cheeks burned as her desire-flooded body got hammered by appalled embarrassment. *Oh, God, I just imagined attraction.* It was one thing to objectify Marco and enjoy watching him as gorgeous eye-candy. It was something else entirely to invent non-verbal signals and imagine he was attracted to her.

Damn it. That went beyond crazy and tipped right into scary.

She knew she wasn't crazy—at least she was fairly certain she wasn't—so she put her inappropriate reaction down to the shock of being dumped by Daniel. That had to be it. Pop psychology would say that her body was reacting to rejection and compensating by wanting to be seen as attractive.

Seriously?

It's all I've got.

To prove to herself that she really was in charge of her body, she jumped to her feet, determined to rescue the uncomfortable moment. 'I was just on my way to see you about Iva. Can you walk and talk?'

'Of course.' He stretched his arm out, the action saying, *After you,* and her body quivered again.

Get over yourself. Plenty of men have good manners.

Name one you know other than William.

But she didn't want to play that game and she didn't want to think about the fact that she'd always used the way William's manners had always made her feel special as a benchmark to measure potential boyfriends against.

Lucy outlined her treatment plan for Iva, and Marco listened, nodding occasionally. 'And now Iva's settled in bed, I have to go and look after Rusty.'

'Excuse me?' His accent rose as he tilted his head and a curl fell onto his forehead making him look like a confused boy rather than a square-jawed, über-professional, doctor-in-charge.

She laughed, but at the same time had to restrain her hand from reaching out and flicking back his hair. 'Iva's dog.'

'He needs the veterinarian?'

'No. I'm looking after him. He just needs some company.'

'Ah, so, this Rusty, is he well-behaved?'

She thought of the aging dog who loved nothing more than having his belly scratched. 'He's a total sweetie, why? Are you worried about me?'

The moment the flirty words tripped unbidden out of her mouth, she wanted to pull them back. She groaned silently, aghast that her body was no longer just content with non-verbal lusting. She kept walking.

He pulled open the door for her, the one that separated the hospital annexe from the main clinic area, and the babbling noise of children's voices rolled towards them. They were happy sounds rather than the crying of sick kids.

Lucy turned back in surprise asking, 'What's going on?' and in the process brushed up against Marco's arm and bumped hard into his chest. His hand shot out to steady her and she suddenly found her fingers splayed against his chest and her forehead resting against his sternum. He smelled of sunshine, leather and a slight hint of antiseptic.

A childhood memory stirred—one of being protected and safe from the world. It was a feeling she hadn't experienced in six, long months and she'd wondered if she'd ever know it again.

She breathed in, this time a long, slow, delicious breath, which not only absorbed his scent, but also the firmness of his chest, the warmth of his skin, and the loud and solid sound of his beating heart. She wanted to stay lost in the memory forever, trapped in a time when life had been so much simpler.

His fingers, which had gently held her with perfect stillness, started moving against her skin with feather-soft touches.

The memory scattered.

Heat built.

This was nothing like the sanctuary of a father's arms. This was the touch of one consenting adult to another and the caresses ignited her blood, making her heart leap. Hot and addictive need pumped through her.

She gasped as his heart jumped to match hers, sending vibrations of unambiguous wanting—his wanting—into every cell of her body. His body called to hers, urging a response, but the call was unnecessary. Her body was already throbbing to the beat of his. Under her palm, his nipple rose, pressing against his shirt. Pressing against her palm. She automatically brushed her thumb over the fine cotton, wishing she was touching skin. His skin.

His soft, guttural groan echoed her heady need, acknowledging it, and a wondrous and teasing ache burned at the apex of her thighs. His heat plundered her body like a wave breaking hard against sand, flattening every shaky defence she'd attempted to build and rendering her legs utterly boneless.

In a blissed-out state, she sank against him, her tingling breasts pressed against his chest, her legs lining his legs, and she tilted her head back, needing to touch his lips.

A new tension in his body pressed hard against her.

Reality ripped into the lust-filled fog that had taken control of her brain.

What are you doing?

With a gut-dropping shock, she realised exactly what she was doing. *Oh, God.* Not only weren't his arms a place of safety and protection—they had danger written all over them. Her head didn't belong on his chest no matter how firm or broad it was or how amazing he felt and smelt, and her hand didn't belong on so intimate an area of the body of a man she barely knew, let alone that they were standing in a very public place. Horrified, she stepped back quickly and her hair fell forward, masking her face. 'Sorry.'

'No problem.'

Hoarseness clung to his words, drawing her gaze to his face like a magnet. Buried in the depths of his chocolate eyes were the not-quite extinguished embers of a raw desire she knew was mirrored in her own. It had hit them both with the velocity of a two tonne truck and he looked as stunned and as shocked as she felt.

If she had a choice, she'd wish herself gone from this uncomfortable situation, but she didn't have magic powers so she was stuck here. *Just deal with it.* She was an adult who had to work with Marco for another few days.

She rolled back her shoulders and faced her embarrassment. 'Seems I'm clumsy today.'

He gave a wry smile which seemed to say, I know what you're doing and thank you. When he finally spoke he said, 'I think your shoes should come with an "unstable" warning.'

She grabbed onto the humour like it was a lifeline and harnessed some faux indignation. 'Hey, my shoes are an occupational necessity. I can't reach the top shelf of the medical supplies room without them.'

He laughed. 'That's what the step-ladder is for. I think you just like pretty shoes and you use your height as an excuse.'

'Tall people never understand.' She tossed her head to hide the zip of surprise which spun in with some discomfort at the fact he'd just read her perfectly. Shoes were her weakness and the source of many burn marks on her credit card.

Keep the focus on work. It's safer.

She walked through the doorway. 'So why all the kid noise?'

Marco kept a firm distance between them. 'Therapy day.'

'Therapy day?' She couldn't recall ever hearing about that from William.

'*Sí.* We host the paediatric clinic once a month and physiotherapy, occupational therapy and speech therapy come to us. It gives the families in the district some relaxation from driving to Geraldton.'

'What a great idea.' Genuine delight rolled through her at his thoughtfulness. 'These families have enough to contend with without adding long-distance travel to the mix.'

'Thank you.'

This time his smile was wide, wreathing his entire face and spilling from his eyes. It was like she'd just bestowed a great compliment on him. Her heart did an odd hiccough-thing. The rest of her wanton body stayed relatively normal.

Thank you! It's about time you started behaving yourself.

'So this Rusty,' Marco said, 'if he is good with children I think they would love to see him.'

She grinned, liking his train of thought. So often, kids with disabilities missed out on the everyday things that able-bodied kids took for granted. 'I'll go and get him and bring him into the waiting room.'

When she reached the truck, Rusty's ears pricked up and he was instantly on his feet, looking at her from over the top of the tray sides. 'Hey, boy.' She rubbed him under his chin. 'Come with me because there's more love like this inside.'

The old dog enthusiastically wagged his tail and with a vigour that belied his age, jumped down from the truck. Trotting by her side, he seemed to smile up at her as they entered the front door of the clinic.

Sue's face stiffened. 'Cattle dogs belong outside.'

Lucy over-smiled in response. She could no longer kid herself that Sue's cool manner toward her was because the nurse was busy or preoccupied—it had been the same each time they'd met. Sue avoided her when she could and when she couldn't, she used a tone filled with condemnation. 'Marco thought the kids might enjoy a dog visit.'

'If he makes a mess, you clean it up.' Sue picked up a ringing telephone, effectively cutting off any reply Lucy might have wanted to make.

She sighed, patted Rusty's head and whispered, 'We're both in the doghouse, mate. Come on, let's go see some kids.'

Given the amount of noise she'd heard ten minutes ago, she was surprised to find only two children waiting and she realised the others must now be in with their therapists having treatment.

Both of the kids were boys. One appeared to be about eight and he was intensely focused on connecting together magnetic sticks in colour-coordinated order. Despite the click-click sound of Rusty's nails on lino, he didn't look up from his task. The other boy was younger with dark hair, and dark eyes which lit up the moment he saw the dog. He stood up and promptly fell backwards onto the chair, as if his legs lacked the strength to hold him.

Lucy took Rusty over and the obliging dog laid his head on the little boy's lap, gazing at him with liquid eyes.

'I'm Lucy and this is Rusty. He loves having his ears scratched.'

Before the child could reply, Sue bustled in and said, 'It's your turn now, Iggie.' She shooed Rusty out of the way and handed the little boy his elbow crutches.

Disappointment burned on the child's face and Lucy moved to reassure him. 'We'll be here when you get back.'

He gave her a shy smile before following Sue, his crutches tapping on the floor.

Lucy watched them leave and turned toward the other child, whose mother had just entered the room. Lucy didn't recognise her and assumed they must live on one of the sheep stations in the district.

The woman bent down next to the child. 'It's time to go, Rob. I'll help you pack up.'

'No.' Rob kept working on his project.

'You can do this with your set as soon as we get home,' his mother beguiled.

'No.' The boy bumped his mother to move her out of the way.

The woman wobbled and shot her hand out to support herself. She looked up at Lucy with a tight and worn-out smile. 'Just once, I'd like him to say, "Yes." I can push it and risk a full-on tantrum or I can sit it out until he's finished.' She sighed. 'It's hard, you know.'

'I'm sure it is.' Lucy really felt for the woman. Based on the child's behaviour, she guessed he might have autism spectrum disorder. She glanced in the large box of magnetic sticks and realised the mother could be in for a bit of a sit if she was going to wait until the box was empty. 'Can I get you a cup of tea and a magazine while you wait for him to finish? You can catch up on the latest celebrity gossip.'

'Thank you. That would be lovely. I'm Janet, by the way.'

'Lucy.' She smiled and then checked how Janet took her tea. Taking Rusty, she walked directly to the kitchen and told the dog to sit by the doorway. As she was searching for the elusive sugar, Marco walked in and immediately dropped down on his haunches, greeting Rusty at eye level. The dog tried to lick him.

Lucy laughed, ignoring the unwanted trill of sensation in the pit of her stomach, and instead concentrated on keeping things light, given what had happened between them twenty minutes ago and what might have happened if she hadn't come to her senses. 'I don't know who's happier to see whom. I'm guessing you have a dog waiting to lavish love on you at home.'

He rubbed noses with the dog. 'Not yet.'

She finally found the sugar in a sealed container in the fridge, having remembered the constant battle Bulla Creek residents waged against ants. 'Why not?'

'I am waiting for the official email from the Department of Immigration telling me I have been granted permanent residency. *That* is the day I get a dog.'

She was intrigued. 'A commitment to Australia?'

'*Sí.* A celebration. The interviews are over and now I wait.'

He rose to his feet and looked at her for the first time since entering the room. A question dominated his warm, brown eyes and she resisted the huge temptation to look beyond it and see if there was any sign of the fire that had burned so brightly earlier.

Marco gave Rusty a final pat. 'I thought you were taking the dog to the children?'

'I am but one of the mums needs some TLC so I'm making her a drink.' She thought about Janet as she stirred the sugar into the tea. 'It must be *so* hard having a kid with a disability. I mean, it's your basic nightmare, really.'

His relaxed demeanour vanished and his jaw tightened, making the end-of-day stubble appear even darker and sexier. He moved abruptly, striding directly to the sink, flicking on the taps with a jerk and tugging overly hard on the liquid soap dispenser. 'All children deserve love.'

The thickly accented words whipped her with unexpected condemnation and she felt the sting all over. 'Of course they do and that's *not* what I meant,' she defended herself. Taking in a deep breath, she pitched for a conciliatory tone. 'But let's be realistic. No expectant parents with their day-dreams of a perfect family would ever put up their hand up for a sick kid. All I'm saying is that it's a basic human desire to have a child who is healthy and normal.'

His large hands yanked on the paper-towels with a vicious pull and about five tumbled out. 'Do you mean disability-free?'

His tone could have cut glass and his animosity hit her hard in the chest. She arced up, cross at being deliberately misconstrued again. 'You can give things politically correct labels but it doesn't change the emotions.'

'Is this our dog?'

Lucy turned toward the young voice and saw the cute, little dark-haired boy on crutches who'd she'd briefly met in the waiting room. He dropped his crutches and threw his arms around a jubilant Rusty. She immediately glanced beyond him, through the doorway and out into the hall, looking for his mother. She couldn't see anyone.

The boy gazed across at Marco, his face alive with animation and with adoration in his eyes. 'Is he?'

Dark, brown eyes the colour of treacle.

Marco's eyes. Marco's curls.

She was staring at Marco's son.

The spoon she was holding fell out of her shocked and numb fingers, clattering loudly onto the stainless steel sink.

Without a glance in her direction, Marco crossed the kitchen and knelt down next to the little boy, tousling his hair. 'No, Ignacio. This dog is just visiting.' He reached for his son's hands. 'We have to go home.'

'But that lady said.' He took in a breath and immense concentration lined his face as he slowly formed each word 'He likes to have. His ears scratched.' Iggie gave her a conspirator's smile. 'Didn't you?'

Before she could reply, Marco had picked up the crutches with one hand and his son with the other. With his shoulders rigid, he turned and walked into the corridor and out of view.

Iggie's loud objections floated back to Lucy.

Marco has a son.

She realised she was now leaning against the sink for support and her brain, usually so quick to grasp information, was lurching and stumbling like a drunk in the dark.

Marco's a father.

She couldn't quite believe it. She thought back to Deb who'd said, 'It's the ones you want that are always the ones you can't have.' Lucy had assumed that was because he was a commitment-phobic bachelor, not because he was married.

No. She shook the thought away, recalling him saying, *he* was waiting to hear from immigration, and there was no way Deb would be after a married man.

Not to mention the two of you almost made out in the corridor.

She thought of Daniel. Being in a relationship didn't stop all men from straying and yet there was something integral about Marco—him being a stickler for rules perhaps—that told her he wouldn't cheat on his wife.

Did all of these titbits of information point to him being a single dad? One thing snagged her—if he was a single dad, why was he doing it alone and so far from his family in Argentina? Especially when his cute-looking son appeared to have cerebral palsy.

It must be so hard having a kid with a disability. I mean, it's your basic nightmare.

She gasped, her hand slapping her mouth as her stomach cramped. Her words, driven by empathy for Janet and spoken so freely a few moments ago, now spread through her like a toxic spill, tainting everything in their path. She'd unwittingly reduced Marco's life and love for his son down to a nightmare.

She wished for all the world she could take those words back.

CHAPTER FIVE

MARCO lay flat on his back on the outdoor table, struggling to find his daily dose of peace that he usually gained from staring up at the night sky. It wasn't working for him. Tonight should have been a fun evening spent with Ignacio, the first early night he'd had in a long time, but Ignacio had been grumpy and difficult all evening, punishing him for the presumptive way he'd picked him up and taken him home without letting him play with the dog. The evening had gone steadily downhill from that point until Ignacio, who was overly tired after his therapy as well as cross with him, had gone to bed. His little boy had even turned his back on his goodnight kiss. Marco had kissed him anyway.

He didn't want to consider that perhaps he'd over-reacted to Lucy. His emotions, usually so ordered and controlled, had been see-sawing erratically from the moment he'd discovered Lucy

Patterson in the office two days ago. Since that moment he'd run the full gauntlet of everything from anger to appreciation, loathing to lust, and a thousand other feelings in between, although if he was honest, he'd let go of his first impression of her after the accident and then when she'd made him laugh. Her blend of strength and fragility fascinated him, drawing him in despite himself. But of all the conflicting emotions that had surged and retreated, none of them had discomposed him more than the moment she'd barrelled into his chest and his arms had insisted on holding her there.

Not since Bianca had he experienced such a strong reaction and even then, those past feelings paled in comparison to what had happened with Lucy. He'd *never* lost control of himself with a woman, but when she'd sagged against him in that doorway, all soft and small as if she needed protection and yet smelling of hot need and unsatisfied hunger, he'd wanted to lift her up against the wall, wrap her legs around his hips and bury himself in her until they were both senseless with greedy satiation.

He ran his hands through his hair, pulling at

the roots. Why now? Why with this particular woman had his body decided to re-find its sex drive? The last time he'd had sex had been just before he'd come to Bulla Creek. He'd been at a conference in Perth and the combination of a wave of unexpected loneliness combined with one glass of wine too many had met with a pretty nurse's flirting and they'd gone up to her room. Even then, his heart hadn't been in it and he'd left soon after, knowing he didn't want any emotional entanglements with any woman. Bianca had burned him for that.

No, his priority was Ignacio and then to the community of Bulla Creek, just like it had been for months.

Yesterday, when William had asked him if he could work with Lucy in the practice, he'd seen her help as a way of claiming back his time for Ignacio and helping William. He'd easily dismissed his zips of attraction to that small, lithe body as momentary aberrations without substance because in the past he'd successfully controlled himself. Today in the corridor those zips had laughed in his face and all previous rafts of desire for her had quadrupled in a heartbeat.

Thankfully, the moments with Lucy in the clinic kitchen had given him an abrupt reprieve from his lust-shaken body. No matter how much he'd thought about having Lucy naked and underneath him, no matter how much she fascinated him, all desire for her had frozen the moment she'd called his beautiful son and his life 'a nightmare'. That bite of reality was enough to restore his equilibrium and he knew it would protect him over the next two days. After that, Lucy Patterson would leave Bulla Creek, William would return to work, the long-awaited email from the Department of Immigration would arrive and he could arrange for his parents to move to Australia. When that happened, then he could really settle into his life in Bulla Creek.

A shooting star whizzed across the sky and he took it as a sign that all would be well and everything would go according to plan. Finally, the calm he'd been seeking descended over him like a cloak and he picked up his phone. He consulted the star guide app and then lifted his binoculars to his eyes, trying to locate another constellation that was new to him despite the light pollution from a full moon.

As he stared at a cluster that was trillions of miles away, he heard a click-click noise and belatedly realised it was the sound of heels tapping on the path that ran along the side of the house.

He'd only just sat up when Rusty appeared, followed by Lucy, who held a large carrier bag. When she saw him on the table, surprise made her brows draw down for a fraction of a second, making her look vulnerable and ill at ease. 'Hello, Marco.'

He jumped on the tiny sparks that tried to flare in response to her mellow voice. 'What are you doing here?'

She bit her lip but held his gaze. 'I came to apologise. I obviously upset you very much and that wasn't my intention at all.'

He stayed seated with his hands pressed against his thighs, trying to keep his composure. He spoke through a stiff jaw. 'My life is *not* a nightmare and neither is my son.'

'No. True. Sorry.' Her mouth pulled down on one side. 'It was a poor choice of words.'

An image of Bianca with a matching sound track played across his mind and he flinched. 'We don't want yours or anyone's pity.'

She stood perfectly still, her knuckles gleaming white in the dark as she gripped the handles of the bag. 'Good, because I wasn't giving it.'

'To me it sounded like you were.'

He tried not to let himself be drawn in by the fall of her hair as it brushed the slight jut of her chin. In the last forty-eight hours he'd noticed far too much about her, including the way she tilted her head back slightly when she was convinced she was right.

She held up the bag and a bottle of wine peeked out of it. 'I bought a peace-offering. Would you be prepared to share a glass with me while I attempt to explain?'

No! Experience had taught him that explanations only gave credence to prejudice and yet despite all that, part of him wanted to hear her talk. He argued out the points in his mind getting nowhere.

Her shoulders slumped slightly at his silence and eventually she put the bag down next to the seat his feet rested on. Rusty sat next to it. She gave the dog a pat and then straightened up. 'I'll just leave the wine here then. I hope you can enjoy it at some other time.'

She cleared her throat while her right hand gripped her left. 'I thought seeing as your son was upset, he might like to wake up to Rusty in the morning. I've got his rug in the bag if you're happy to have him for the night.'

He'd been able to withstand her attempt at an apology and the wine, but the ice around Marco's heart softened slightly at this unanticipated thoughtfulness. 'Ignacio would like that very much.'

Say goodbye now. He reached down and picked up the bag and glass clinked against glass, surprising him. 'You brought glasses?'

She shrugged but again she didn't shy away from his gaze. 'Glasses, wine, cheese and grapes. The full apology.'

He read real regret in her eyes and he found himself over-ruling his previous decision. 'It would be ill-mannered of me then not to share it with you.'

Without moving from the table, he opened the bottle and poured the wine before holding out a glass. As she accepted it, her fingers brushed his lightly and the touch streaked through him like a hot wind, flaming the embers of his barely banked desire.

Hold fast to what she said.

She raised her glass in his direction. 'Marco, when you came in yesterday I was making tea for a completely stressed out mother who'd just told me how hard things are for her. My comments to you were driven by empathy for her. Her life is harder because of her son's disability.'

He shook his head. 'Her life is different from what it might have been but that does not make it the nightmare you believe.'

She sighed and tucked her hair behind her left ear. 'The expression "your basic nightmare" isn't literal. It means something you don't really want to have happen. I doubt that Janet's experience of parenthood is what she would have expected before Rob was born.'

He thought of his marriage to Bianca and immediately took a gulp of wine. '*Sí*, but everyone's reaction to that experience is different.'

'Absolutely. On that we agree.'

Only that still didn't tell him where she stood on the prejudice scale for people with disabilities or if she even did. Had he misunderstood an

Australian colloquialism? He was trying to work it all out when she swung up next to him on the table. Her scent eddied around him in the cooler night air and was even more alluring than in the heat of the day. He steeled himself—on guard against his body's reaction of an addictive surge of primal need.

A ripple ran through him, calling him to follow.

Lucy set down her glass next to her and handed him a small bunch of grapes before helping herself to some. 'I didn't know you were a father until your son appeared in the kitchen. Is he your only child?'

'My one and only.'

'Tell me about him.'

He pulled the grapes off the now-brittle vine and thought about his little boy who slept only metres away in a bedroom decorated with posters of action heroes. 'Ignacio is five and in his first year at school.'

'Sue called him Iggie. Do you?'

Her question surprised him. After their earlier conversation he'd expected her to go straight to, 'Is his diagnosis cerebral palsy?' 'I call him Ignacio, but everyone else in town calls him Iggie. It is the Australian way I think, to shorten a name.'

She laughed a husky rough-throated sound which was at complete odds with her petite frame and feminine curves. It rolled through him, overtaking the previous ripple and bringing with it visions of tangled sheets and hot, sweaty bodies. He slammed grapes into his mouth, trying to concentrate exclusively on chewing.

She stared straight ahead. 'You're right. We shorten a long name and lengthen a short one. Does Ignacio like being called Iggie?'

'He does.' He thought about how desperate his son was to fit in. 'He likes anything that makes him feel like he's the same as the other kids in his class.'

She tilted her head back and dropped a grape into her mouth. His gaze zeroed in on her slender alabaster neck, pulled there by a force greater than his resistance. When she swallowed, his groin tightened.

None of this is wise.

He made himself look away.

She twirled her glass and the moonlight danced in the reflections. 'I remember when I was in my first year at Bulla Creek Primary and everyone was asked to bring in a picture of their brother or sister for show and tell. I'd been asking for a baby brother or sister for a year so the request really hit me because I was the only child in the class of thirty without a sibling. I didn't want to be singled out by not having a photo so I took a picture of our dog. It back-fired and I still get teased by people who were in that class.'

He felt himself smile. 'It is not such a bad thing to be an only child. I have two brothers and all I wanted was a room to myself.'

She turned to look at him, her grey eyes huge in her face and filled with an understanding that had nothing to do with either of their unmet wants about siblings. She spoke softly. 'At that age we hate anything that marks us as different.'

He nodded. 'Right now Ignacio hates his crutches.'

He heard himself speaking the words, stunned he was telling her because he hadn't shared this thought with anyone, not even Ignacio's therapists who he occasionally confided in.

She gazed up at the sky. 'Of course he does,

but it's better that he hates his crutches rather than his legs.'

He mulled over her words as the complex flavours of the merlot rolled over his tongue and he realised with a jolt that he hadn't thought about Ignacio and his crutches in those terms. The words made it sound like a subtle difference, but in fact it was the complete opposite. It momentarily eased the permanent ache in his heart for the struggle his son faced every day of his life.

Lucy stared up at the night sky, idly thinking it had been far too long since she'd stargazed. Marco sat next to her, silent and brooding, and although she had no clue what he was thinking, she'd sensed a shift in his attitude toward her. At least he was no longer furious and he'd listened to her try and dig herself out of an off-the-cuff comment. She must remember that despite his excellent English, some expressions might confuse him and she didn't want or need another misunderstanding like this one. She had no emotional energy left to deal with situations like this when she still had all the stuff with William hanging about like a massive elephant in the room.

Granted, she hadn't spent much time at Haven,

although she'd cooked a meal for him tonight but had left soon after to come here. Over dinner, William's conversation had been centred on the food, the weather and the arrangements for the removal of his cast. Was he waiting for her to talk to him? Just thinking about it gave her a tight throat and wet eyes and she wasn't ready to say anything.

Lucy broke the silence. 'I'd forgotten how amazing the stars are up here.'

Marco lifted his head and his smile lacked the tightness that had clung to his lips when she'd arrived. 'I was lying down looking at them when you arrived.'

'Ah! So that's why you're sitting on the table?'

'*Sí*. It's much easier on the neck. Try it.'

The idea appealed and she set her glass down on the seat out of harm's way and then lay down. Unbidden, a sigh rolled out of her as she lost herself in the world of space. 'A purist would say the moon's too bright and it isn't worth looking tonight, but I disagree. What's that?'

Marco's dark head followed the direction of her arm. 'Let me check.' He held his phone up in the direction she was pointing and then lay down next to her, his movements very controlled as if he was determined not to touch her.

She hated the disappointment that scudded through her.

'That is Betelgeuse.' He touched the information button and all the technical details appeared. 'It's a red supergiant.'

'That's a totally awesome app. I'll have to tell Da—' She stopped herself, not wanting to think about the times she'd used William's telescope. 'Can I try it?'

'Sure.'

She held it up in the direction she'd been looking and kept moving the phone but the screen spun unable to settle on anything. 'I can't find it.'

'You need to go more slowly.'

She kept trying but without success and eventually Marco slid his palm over the back of her hand and his arm entwined with hers. His touch spread through her like caramel sauce—hot, sweet and never enough—and with gentle pressure, he moved her hand slowly and steadily until the name of the star cluster appeared.

She struggled to concentrate on the stars as his warmth slowly stripped her brain of cognitive thought. 'So if I do this—' She moved the phone carefully and his hand stayed with hers.

'You are now looking at Sirius in Canis Major. It looks like a big dog.'

'This is so cool.' She lowered her arm and his came down with it. Their hands rested on top of each other in the space between them. The touch was completely passive; no linking of fingers, no movement, just the back of her hand sitting against his palm and yet it burned into every part of her with a fiery grip as if his fingers were actually crushing hers.

She turned her head and her hair brushed against his shoulder. 'Thank you for showing me that.'

He met her gaze, his eyes as dark as the night. 'You're welcome.'

Time to look back at the stars.

But his eyes held hers with hypnotic control. Silence enveloped them, except she could hear the erratic thumping of her heart as loud as an amplified bass-beat.

His breath fanned her face and all she had to do was move her head a fraction and her lips would brush his. God, she wanted to move. She wanted to know if his full lips would cushion hers in softness or press firmly against them before his tongue entered her mouth with coaxing need. She wanted to learn if he tasted of the fire she'd seen bright in his eyes earlier and experience the moment it lit through her and merged with her own in an explosion of sheer tingling and wondrous bliss. But mostly she wanted to feel his arms tight around her again so she could lose herself in them and forget everything.

Instant gratification comes with regrets. His lips might be cool, he might taste of rejection and his arms might not want you.

But her body throbbed in time to the beat of an internal drum that called her to risk it all.

He swallowed.

A low moan left her lips.

She didn't know who moved first. Their lips met in a clash of unleashed need which seared her to her core. His taste of mulberry and mocha filled her mouth followed by a fireball of desire that rocked her to her toes. His left hand roamed over her and his right hand cupped her neck, pulling her closer.

She buried her hand into his thick hair, needing

to touch him, and his phone dug into her leg. She didn't care. All she knew was that she wanted to line his body with hers and feel him pressing against every part of her. Her breasts flattened against his chest and her nipples—grazed by the confines of her bra—ached so hard to touch his skin they hurt.

His knee nudged between her legs and she slid hers over his, welcoming the weight of his thigh firm against her hot, wet and throbbing place that was now calling all the shots, and controlling her with a strength she'd never experienced before.

She willingly surrendered to it.

His tongue plundered her mouth, meeting hers, and together they duelled, fighting to dominate and lay claim to their equal need. She couldn't get enough of his taste, his touch, his pressure and her head spun so fast she risked blacking out.

At the same moment they broke away to breathe, their chests heaving and gasping for breath.

They stared at each other, stunned.

The moment extended beyond a long breath. Beyond two. Her body sobbed, demanding she kiss him again, kiss him right now, but something held her back from slamming her mouth against his where it so wanted to be.

His fingers trailed a deliciously slow path from the back of her neck and along her jaw until his thumb gently brushed her swollen lips. As the touch—so calm and controlled compared to the frenzy of a moment ago—spiralled through her, his eyelids lowered, shutting her out. Distancing himself from her.

A chill washed through her.

'*Papá!* I'm thirsty.' Ignacio's sleepy voice called out from inside the house.

'I have to go.'

Marco's hoarse words said it all but when his hand fell away from her and he sat up, their separation was complete.

She sat up as well and somewhere through the thickness of the heady need that made her limbs heavy and her mind slow, she managed to find her voice. 'Yeah, of course.'

'I'm sorry, Lucy. This is…' He ran his hand through his hair and let out a ragged breath. 'My priority is my son.'

'Of course he is. Don't be sorry.' She managed a dry laugh as she fingered her rumbled hair back into place. 'I just broke up with someone so this is all way too fast and too soon. Besides, I'm heading back to Perth in a couple of days and I won't be back.' A tug of something she didn't want to name made her add, 'Not often anyway.'

He picked up his phone and then slid to his feet, his demeanour now professional and distant. 'So I will see you at the clinic in the morning?'

She stood up, shaking her head slowly as her unease about tomorrow curdled in her gut. 'No, I'm taking William to Geraldton to have his cast removed, unless of course you want to take him and I'll run the clinic? You might enjoy a change of pace.'

He frowned. 'You're family so it is best that you go. I don't know what has gone wrong between you two but perhaps the time together in the car will help?'

'*Nothing* is going to help.' She crossed her arms to stop the tremble that threatened to roll through her and spill tears. 'I'll be back by late afternoon so you can get home earlier and I'll be on call for any evening emergencies.'

'Thank you. I appreciate that.'

A moment ago they'd been about to tear each

other's clothes off and now they were being so polite she thought she'd crack from the strain. 'Not a problem at all.'

She expected him to leave. She *needed* him to leave, but he stood there watching her and she grew hot under his gaze.

'Papá!'

She glanced toward the house. 'He's sounding upset. You should go and take Rusty with you.'

His whole body jerked. *'Sí. Buenas noches.* Goodnight, Lucy.'

Goodnight, Marco. She nodded, watching him leave, hearing the crash of the wire door closing behind him and the dog, and then her wobbly legs gave way and she sat down on the hard seat.

Well done. You're both being sensible.

So why did it feel like she'd just severed a limb?

CHAPTER SIX

'DOES it feel odd?' Lucy's hands gripped the steering wheel as she took a quick glance at William's leg, which was now devoid of a cast and muscle wasting was obvious.

'It feels a lot lighter.' William's voice sounded tired. 'The physio put me through my paces and it's aching a bit now.'

'Do you want some ibuprofen? You could take it with the leftover salad roll?'

'No, I can wait until dinner.'

They were close to home. She'd treated the day as being a carer for William because it gave her the detachment she needed to cope. They'd discussed articles they'd both read in medical journals, her surgery rotation in Perth and William's perspective on the future health needs of Bulla Creek. They'd finally lapsed into silence and let music fill the space. 'I won't be home for dinner. Seeing I've been AWOL most of the day, I'm going to finish up for Marco.'

'I'm glad the two of you get along.'

Sadness tinged his words and the unspoken message was, *We used to get along*.

She blocked it, refusing to go there and thought instead of Marco. The memory of being pressed hard against him with her tongue deep in his mouth, greedily tasting, slammed through her making her cheeks burn.

Bad move.

She cleared her throat. 'We do okay.' *Change the topic*. 'You didn't mention he had a little boy.'

'You didn't ask.' The words carried a quiet note of condemnation, one that said, *You don't talk to me any more*. 'Iggie's a delight. He can out-race me on his crutches, but that's not unexpected. I'm slowing down.'

William had always been a powerhouse of energy and she shrugged off his words. 'Now the cast's off, you'll progress quickly.'

'You were sitting next to me when Jeremy Lucas said not to overdo things. I've decided to take another couple of weeks off so I can return at full power.'

His decision surprised her but it also gave her a

perfect opportunity. 'Is this anything to do with the blood pressure medication you're taking?'

William sucked in a sharp breath. 'There's nothing wrong with my blood pressure.'

She slowed as a kangaroo hopped across the road. 'I saw the tablets in the pantry.'

'They're not mine.'

She didn't believe him. 'Then what are they doing in the pantry?'

'I can't quite bring myself to throw them out just yet.'

This time grief threaded through his words and tried to catch her, but she wouldn't allow it. Relief that he wasn't sick got tangled up with her own grief and ever-present anger with Ruth. 'I didn't realise she'd been taking medication. I'm glad you don't have hypertension but is taking more time off fair to Marco?'

'It is if you stay, unless of course Daniel can't bear to be without you?'

'We broke up.' The words slipped out automatically, breaking the self-imposed rule she'd made the day of Ruth's funeral to no longer share any of her life with William. Stealing her get-out-of-Bulla-Creek card.

'Good.' William sounded the happiest she'd heard him since she'd arrived. 'He was too smooth by half and he lacked heart. So with no real ties in Perth you *can* stay longer.'

She stared straight ahead hating that 'no ties' pretty much summed up her situation. She didn't belong anywhere. Her roots had been unceremoniously ripped up and were yet to be replanted. Gritting her teeth she said, 'I wasn't planning on a working holiday.'

'But you enjoy the work?'

Lucy saw the two kilometre sign flash past, heralding how close they were to Bulla Creek. So close in distance and yet so far in seconds. She swallowed against the acid that burned the back of her throat. 'There was never any doubt I'd enjoy the work but *you* know why I can't stay here.'

'What if I said this was the last thing I'll ever ask of you?'

His quietly spoken words packed a punch. She'd avoided William for months and now he was giving her the perfect out. Do time and then cut her ties for good. It should have brought relief but instead she felt desperately sad.

William continued quietly. 'If not for me, Lucy,

then do it for Marco. He's a good bloke working hard at being a sole parent with the added strain of Iggie's CP. He's a damn fine doctor and Bulla Creek needs him.'

And utterly sexy and totally unavailable.

Her fingers had been gripping the steering wheel so hard they cramped. She was torn. Neither staying nor leaving was palatable as each option came with its own set of demons. In Perth she was alone. It wasn't going to take three weeks to move house and did she really want to return to work early just to deal with hospital gossip and faces filled with curiosity and pity? No, that wasn't tempting in the least, but the other choice was staying in Bulla Creek. Two more weeks going hot, cold and tingly, and lusting after a man she shouldn't want and couldn't have.

Things in her life just kept getting better and better.

A surge of bitterness burned her. 'I thought I knew you, William, but now I realise I never did. You have the soul of a blackmailer.'

He flinched. 'Is that a "yes"?'

You can continue to work huge days with no time to think.

'I'll stay two more weeks but I'm only doing it to give Marco time with his son.'

William didn't reply and the music rolled out between them filling the pain-filled space.

As she slowed to turn off the main road, William asked, 'Have you heard from your mother, Lucy?'

His question sliced through her, ripping away any scabs that had tried to form over the weeping wound that was her heart. 'Not yet.'

'I hope for your sake that you do.'

Her neck jerked around so fast and hard it hurt, but if she'd heard understanding in his voice, his profile was taut with tension. 'You told me trying to contact her was a betrayal of Ruth.'

Sadness ringed him. 'We've both said things we regret, Lucy.'

'You can only speak for yourself, not for me.' She pulled up outside Haven, his duplicity still gripping her as strong as ever. Her need to flee made her heart beat faster. She jumped out of the car, strode around to the boot, grabbed William's walking stick and got to his door just as he stood up.

He swayed slightly and gripped the top of the door to steady himself.

She shoved the aid into his hand as the doctor in her came to the fore. 'Here. You need this to help with your balance. I've left your dinner in the fridge and remember to take some analgesia with it.'

William took a few steps, his hazel eyes dark with shadows. 'Is it always going to be like this?'

She refused to let him draw her into that conversation so instead moved ahead of him and slid her key into the old lock on the front door. As he walked through the doorway she said, 'If you do your physio you should be off the stick within six weeks.'

He stamped the cane on the old hardwood floors. 'Damn it. You're my daughter, Lucy, not my doctor.'

She tilted her chin, keeping her tears at bay. 'Right now being your doctor is the *only* thing I can be.'

Before he could reply she stepped back onto the veranda and closed the door behind her.

Marco was on his way back from his last appointment, a home visit to an elderly patient where he'd been held up waiting for the ambulance. It was the worst night for it to happen because Heather had a family birthday and wasn't available to collect Ignacio. After-school care had rung to say they were closing and they'd arranged for Ignacio to go to the clinic. Marco knew Sue would have him set up doing jigsaw puzzles or listening to talking books and that he'd be fine, but it made it a long day for a little boy who was always physically exhausted even after a normal day.

As he approached the clinic, he slowed, driving past the oval where the Bulla Creek junior footballers were working hard at their training session. He was still trying to get used to the Australian Rules Football code and accept the fact that what he called 'football', Australians called 'soccer'. Soccer wasn't big in Bulla Creek although a few parents at the primary school— mostly mothers—were trying to generate interest and field a team because it was a game that generally came with fewer injuries. Emily, who had one son who played football and another who played soccer, had asked him to give a talk about it at a parent evening. He'd accepted the invitation and pushed down his heartache that Ignacio wouldn't be playing either sport.

The soccer nets were adjacent to the oval and not often used so he was surprised to see in the distance what looked like a mother and her child. The kid stood in front of the goal and the woman was doing a fair job of kicking the ball to him while a dog charged around them both. He squinted against the setting sun, trying to work out who it was.

His foot hit the brake.

He looked again and shook his head at the silhouettes. *You are imagining things.*

For six long days he'd been imagining things—things he and Lucy Patterson could do dressed and naked, in a bed, on a desk, almost anywhere, and it left him feeling permanently strung out and frazzled. When he'd taken William's phone call telling him that Lucy was working at the clinic for two more weeks he'd almost said no.

Help like that was no help at all, not when it slammed up against his sanity every moment of the day and night.

If he was honest, the only thing testing his sanity right now was his imagination because he'd hardly seen Lucy since the night in his garden. It was as if by mutual agreement they were giving each other a wide berth. A very wide berth. Only right now he was certain he was looking straight at her. And Ignacio. It made no sense at all.

He parked and jogged around the dusty edge of the oval. As he approached, the orange light of the setting sun lit up Lucy's hair like a beacon as well as illuminating the sweet curves of her breasts and behind. Shocks of pleasure detonated and he tingled with the memory of her body pressed hard against his.

Surprise collided with it. He didn't recognise her shoes. Instead of her usual platform wedges or high-heeled stilettos, she wore flat, white, sports shoes. He hadn't thought such utilitarian footwear existed in her collection.

Beyond her, at the edge of the goal net was the familiar sight of his little boy who stood with a slight lean to the left. His face was fierce with concentration and his eyes were fixed on the black and white ball at Lucy's feet.

She kicked the ball and Ignacio blocked it with his crutch. A wide grin wreathed the little boy's face as he punched the air with his right hand.

A lump formed in Marco's throat.

Lucy cheered as she moved forward to pick up the ball.

Ignacio suddenly saw him. *'Papá!'*

Lucy spun around as Marco closed the gap between them and he saw the moment she locked down the need—desire generated by the exact same memory that had just rolled through him.

He concentrated his gaze on his son, hugging him close. *'Querido* that was a good block.'

Ignacio squirmed out of his arms and said, 'I've done it. Five times. Haven't I, Lucy?'

'You have.' Her smile for Ignacio shone as bright as the setting sun.

'That is a great job. Like I told you…' he tousled his Ignacio's curls '…your crutches are your friend.'

The little boy pouted. 'I want to kick the ball.'

Lucy handed the ball to Marco who set it down in front of Ignacio wondering how this would go and if he could coordinate the kick to hit the ball, let alone the centre. 'Give it your best shot.'

'You and Lucy need…' Ignacio pointed as he took a breath '…to stand over there.'

Marco hesitated but Lucy walked about ten

metres away. He frowned. There was no way Ignacio would be able to kick the ball that far.

'Marco,' Lucy called out to him and beckoned with her hand.

'Go, *Papá*.'

He unhappily crossed the short distance and as he reached Lucy, he turned to see Ignacio's gaze fixed intently on the boys playing football.

His son dropped his crutches.

'Ignacio.' Marco heard the sternness in his voice as he moved forward.

Lucy's hand touched his arm, pulling him back. 'Let him try.'

He shook her hand away. 'He will fall over.'

'Is that a bad thing?'

He stared at her, stunned. 'You want him to fail?'

'I want him to *try*.'

Apprehension for his beautiful son morphed with love and protection. 'Ignacio, use your crutches.'

Black curls bounced in defiance and his small shoulders moved forward as he drew his leg back, the toe of his shoe dragging in the dirt. With huge effort, he moved his leg forward toward the ball but his left leg crumpled underneath him, bringing him down in a heap before his right foot could connect.

'*Querido Dios.*' Marco moved quickly. 'Are you hurt?' He ran his hands over Ignacio's legs.

'I'm okay. *Papá*, Stop it.' He batted Marco's hands away. 'I want to. Try again.'

'It's getting late, Iggie.' Lucy's voice was both calm and firm as she pointed to the oval. 'The other boys are stopping too because it's almost dark and it's time for dinner. Rusty and I are starving but we can do this again another day.'

Iggie's face lit up with hope. 'Tomorrow, Lucy? Please.'

Lucy kept her gaze fixed on Ignacio. 'Your dad's free tomorrow afternoon so he can bring you here.'

'*Papá* doesn't know…' he breathed in '…how to kick a ball.'

'What?' Marco heard the defensiveness in his voice. 'Of course I can kick a ball. Why would you say that?'

Dark eyes as familiar to him as his own met his. 'You never kick. A ball with me. Not like Lucy.'

Because you fall over. Marco's heart twisted, only the pain wasn't solely the etched-in heartache for his son's constant battle with his limitations. With a shock, he realised he was jealous. Jealous that Ignacio was looking beyond him for experiences and finding him lacking.

'Come on, mate. On your feet.' Lucy bent down and picked up the crutches.

I am his father. A surge of irritation scratched him inside and out. Marco scooped Ignacio into his arms and swung him up and onto his shoulders, holding him firmly by the waist. 'He's tired and it's a long walk to the car.'

His son laughed the way he always did when he rode up high on his shoulders and Marco's world levelled out again. He knew Ignacio. Only he knew what he needed and he definitely knew what was best for him. Lucy had no clue. 'Sue usually does jigsaws with him.'

Lucy heard the disapproval in Marco's voice which matched the deep scowl on his face, one that could summon thunder. Last time she'd seen it he'd accused her of prejudice against people with disabilities. That accusation could no longer be levelled at her and yet he was upset with her again. Everyone in town said he was easy-going, but with her he was all over the place; polite one minute, cross the next, laughing with her or kissing her senseless.

He's struggling with this crazy attraction as much as you are.

Poor guy. I know how he feels.

The thought was somehow gratifying and despite almost getting a crick in her neck, she made herself meet his eyes from her flat-shoed stance. She refused to apologise for choosing the ball activity to entertain Iggie. 'Sadly, Sue couldn't stay late tonight and as I'd cleared the waiting room of patients, I offered to help out. It's too nice an evening to be indoors and with the summer heat arriving soon, it seemed a shame to waste it.'

'Thank you for minding him.' The polite response seemed to be wrung out of him, as if he wasn't thankful at all.

She swallowed a sigh and held out the ball. 'Here you go. You guys will need this for tomorrow.'

Marco's mouth firmed into a grim line as his eyes rolled upwards to indicate the fact that he was gripping his son firmly, supporting the little boy's core muscles so he could remain upright, and that Iggie was holding on tightly to Marco's neck.

There were no extra hands to hold a ball.

She felt stupid for not realising but at the same time resentful that Marco seemed to be making her out to be the bad guy. It was beyond obvious he thought she'd overstepped the mark by choosing a ball-game activity but she knew Iggie had enjoyed it right up until Marco had wanted to control the game. Granted, trying to kick a ball at the end of the day wasn't the best timing, but the kid had guts and determination which counted for a lot. Did Marco recognise that?

It was clear as the outback sky that he loved his son dearly, but she couldn't help but wonder if he was over-protecting the little boy.

'Marco! Lucy!' Emily ran over panting. 'James Audrey's hurt.'

'I'll go,' Lucy offered.

Marco shook his head. 'I have my bag in the car which will save five minutes.'

'Both of you go,' Emily said, 'and I'll mind Iggie.' She held out her arms out for Ignacio with a proprietary air, as if she'd done it many times before.

Lucy experienced an odd sensation that she couldn't name, but she had no time to second-guess it. She started running.

'Excuse me, boys.' Lucy moved through the circle of people who'd gathered around the twelve-year-old boy. James lay on the ground, his face ashen and tight, and despite his heroic efforts, a tear rolled down his cheek. His left hand held his right arm slightly away from his side as if he was guarding it. 'Are his parents here?'

The coach held a mobile phone. 'I'm trying to contact them now.'

'Thanks.' She knelt down beside the boy. 'James, my name's Lucy and I'm a doctor. In a minute another doctor, Marco, will be here with his medical bag. Tell me, where does it hurt?'

'My arm.'

'Does it hurt worse in one place than another?'

His finger's crawled to his shoulder and he flinched. 'It's really bad here but it hurts everywhere,' he sobbed.

'Do you remember which part of your body hit the ground first?'

'No. It really hurts.'

'Did you hit your head? Black out?'

James shook his head and flinched again. 'No.'

'Okay, then let's see what you've done to yourself.' She had her suspicions but her time in emergency medicine had taught her that a thorough examination meant she didn't miss something important by jumping feet first to a diagnosis. Carefully running her hand along his lower arm, she felt for a break in the radius and ulna. Nothing. She gently continued up the arm but couldn't feel the distinctive lump of a break on the humerus either.

James moaned.

'Does this hurt more than the lower part of your arm?'

'Yes and your fingers feel fuzzy.'

'Is your arm numb?'

'Sorta.'

Radiating pain and numbness matched her initial suspicions and things firmed up the moment she examined his shoulder. Instead of looking round, it looked square with a bump under the skin. The head of the humerus was no longer in the glenoid fossa and instead was lying anteriorly. At twelve, dislocated shoulders were not that common and the tenderness along the humerus worried her.

She glanced up to greet Marco's arrival. 'Dislocated shoulder and possible fracture of the humerus.'

'Poor kid.' He did a set of observations and then handed the boy the 'green whistle', the emergency painkiller of choice for haemodynamically stable patients. 'James, I want you to suck on this and it will help you with the pain. Take a couple of deep breaths to start with.'

The boy accepted the whistle and sucked in a long breath, happy to do anything that might help. Lucy ran through their treatment options. 'He's got severe pain and I'm not convinced that there isn't damage to the head of the humerus, so I want an X-ray before I try to pop his shoulder back.'

Marco looked thoughtful. 'By the time you move him to the clinic and do the X-ray, the muscle spasm will mean he'll need a light anaesthetic for the reduction.'

'I know but it will be a lot less painful for James all round.' Lucy scanned the oval looking for running parents but they hadn't arrived. 'We need his parents' permission for the procedure so we keep him as comfortable as we can until they arrive.'

'Of course.' Marco suddenly sighed and his expression tensed.

'Problem? You're not comfortable doing the anaesthetic?'

He shook his head. 'The medicine isn't the problem. It's the timing. Why does everything happen when Heather is unavailable?' He ran his hands through his hair. 'I suppose I could ask Emily to take Ignacio to her place.'

He didn't sound keen on the idea and despite the fact he'd been so disapproving of the way she'd entertained his son, she found herself saying, 'William's a five minute drive away and he not only loves kids, he's great with them. Take Iggie to Haven and they can keep each other company.'

His deep forehead creased in thought. 'But that leaves you here with James.'

She laughed. 'I'm a big girl, Marco, and all I'm doing is observations and waiting for the ambulance. You'll probably get back at much the same time as James arrives at the hospital.'

He had the grace to look slightly sheepish. 'I'm not sure I'm totally deserving of your help.'

She grinned. 'Probably not, but it's William who's doing the helping and right now he's not kicking any balls.'

'This is true.'

His wry smile washed over her like a sunbeam and her blood instantly heated, pumping through her hard and fast, carrying with it the addictive need that refused to fade no matter the instructions she gave herself.

James groaned. Lucy's attention snapped toward her patient, thankful she had a reason to look away from those dark, dark eyes that always called to her to abandon all common sense. 'You okay, mate?'

'I think I'm gonna throw up.'

And he did.

CHAPTER SEVEN

MARCO found Lucy in the clinic kitchen. 'James is awake and his parents are with him.'

'Great. And almost as good is that I've just finished up his report.' She shot Marco a smile filled with the companionship of a job shared and done well.

Something inside him shifted and he found himself needing to clear his throat. 'All that pain and the poor boy does not even get the status symbol of wearing a cast.'

'I'll make sure he goes home tomorrow with a permanent marker so his mates can sign his cuff and collar sling.'

The more he worked with Lucy, the more he realised she did little things like this all the time. Thoughtful things like caring for an old man's dog.

Bringing the dog around so Ignacio could spend time with him.

He held up a mug. 'Drink?'

Astonishment flared in her eyes. 'You're not heading straight to Haven?'

He shook his head, having learned the drill of single parenthood years ago. 'William texted to say Ignacio fell asleep on the couch so I am eating first and collecting Ignacio second or it will be another hour before I get anything to eat.'

Understanding crossed her face. 'Good idea. The few friends I have with children tell me that you use the time they're asleep wisely.' She pushed up from the chair. 'I'm starving too so I'll join you.'

It was his turn to be surprised. 'I thought you would be going to Haven?'

'And risk waking Ignacio before you arrive?' The tension that often ringed her shot back in and she gave him a tight smile. 'I wouldn't do that to you. Tell you what, after all that drama I need chocolate. If you make me a hot chocolate I'll cook.'

He had a very strong feeling that her not going home had nothing to do with waking his son. Ever since that first lunch with William and Lucy, he'd been hoping they could sort out whatever it was that had put them at odds. It didn't appear to be working. Neither William nor Lucy had spoken to him about the problem and as much as he wondered about it, he hadn't asked because it wasn't strictly his business. He'd got the help he needed and the less he knew about Lucy, the more protection he had in trying to keep his distance from her. It fortified his defences, preventing him from succumbing to the ever-present urge to haul her hard against his chest and kiss her senseless.

He rolled his eyes and said, 'Reheating a frozen meal in the microwave is hardly cooking.'

She laughed and her whole body seemed to relax as she opened the freezer to the stack of healthy meals that Susan and Felicity kept stocked. 'And yet all too often it's as close to cooking as I get.'

He remembered his early years of being a doctor. 'Residency is a crazy life.'

The beep of the microwave buttons echoed around the kitchen. 'So it's like that in Argentina too?'

'*Sí*. Hard years of long hours.'

He made the drinks and she accepted the steaming mug of chocolate, breathing in the rich scent. A look of bliss washed over her face.

The image of her naked and sprawled across his bed, with an even better expression on her face slammed into him, making him hard. He gulped his tea. *Dios.* The hot drink burned his mouth as much as his blood burned with his need. He flicked on the tap, filled a glass with water and downed it fast, trying to cool his body.

'You okay?'

Her breathy voice matched his heat-filled body and did nothing to help him wrestle back some control, but he managed to grind out, 'Fine.'

She bit her lip and centred her gaze at a point somewhere over his shoulder. 'I sometimes think that instant hot water isn't a good idea and we should go back to tea and coffee out of a pot.'

He grabbed onto her throwaway line, happy to have a safe and boring conversation during which he could re-find his equilibrium. 'I will buy a coffee machine.'

'Great idea.'

He opened the cutlery drawer, picked up the knives and forks and set the table. When he glanced up, she was staring at him, her warm, grey eyes filled with questions.

'We were talking about medicine in Argentina.'

'Ah, yes, we were.' He smiled. Talking about work was safe. 'What do you want to know?'

'Why you've made a permanent move to Australia?'

The unexpected question reverberated through him and he watched the meals going around and around in the microwave while he carefully formulated his reply. 'It was necessary.'

She diced some salad. 'Necessary how?'

The microwave conveniently beeped, thankfully diverting Lucy's attention. She carefully spooned out generous portions of beef in red wine casserole into pasta bowls and Marco sliced some ciabatta loaf, adding it to a plate in the centre of the table.

He sat opposite her, needing the width of the table between them to avoid any unintentional touching because it wouldn't take much for him to push all his reasons aside and pull her into his arms. The serving of the meal had broken the conversation he didn't want to have and he was determined to start a new topic. A topic that had nothing to do with him.

He took a mouthful of the food. 'This tastes okay but you haven't lived until you've tasted Argentine beef cooked to succulent perfection on the barbeque.'

She dunked a piece of bread in the jus. 'So you were saying that leaving Argentina was necessary. As you're practising medicine I assume you weren't run out of the country for criminal activity.' The smile in her voice was underpinned by an edge of determination.

He swore silently. She had no intention of talking about food. 'I am sorry to disappoint you but it was nothing so interesting.'

Curiosity flared in her pretty eyes. 'Try me.'

He shrugged, trying to keep things very casual. 'Bulla Creek is a fresh start for Ignacio and me.'

'And?'

'And nothing. I think Bulla Creek is a good place...' he smiled at her '...but I don't need to tell you that because you grew up here. Ignacio loves the library and the pool. What did you like most about the town when you were a kid?'

Frustration played around her kissable mouth. 'Marco, why did you need a fresh start?'

He gripped his fork tightly, feeling the same surge of anger and betrayal that flared every time he thought about his marriage to Bianca. Feelings he badly wanted to banish but he couldn't seem to manage just yet. 'I am divorced.'

Her eyes widened. 'Oh. I…'

His jaw ached with tightness. 'Thought I would be a widower?'

'I did. Sorry.'

The fury inside deposited there by Bianca burned brightly. 'Sorry for what? That my wife is not dead?' The unjust words left his mouth before he could pull them back.

She blinked, but kept her gaze steady. 'There's no right way to answer that question, Marco, and I don't want to pick a fight with you.' She gave him a quiet smile and opened her palms. 'I'm sorry you're hurting and I'm sorry your marriage failed. Not that I've been married but I can't imagine anyone ever enters into it wanting it to fail.'

His fury faded under her empathy and he

sighed. 'I'm sorry. What I said was unfair and you're right. I didn't want my marriage to fail.'

She twirled her fork around the bowl. 'So you got divorced after you arrived in Australia?'

He picked up his empty plate and stood up needing to move as memories crowded in on him. 'No, I got divorced in Argentina.'

Her forehead creased. 'So where's your ex-wife living?'

He stowed the bowl in the dishwasher. 'Bianca remains in Buenos Aires specialising in infectious diseases and affairs.' He slammed the dishwasher shut. 'She was very good at that.'

The sympathy in her eyes suddenly cooled and her chin rose as did her voice. 'So your fresh start is separating Ignacio from his mother to punish her?'

Bitterness burned the back of his throat. 'This is nothing about punishment. Ignacio is better off without her in his life.'

Lucy's face twisted in pain. 'Adults might think they're acting in the best interest of the child by denying access but, believe me, a child needs to have contact with his parents. *Both* his parents.'

His chest burned at the unfairness of life and

he stared down at her, peppering her with words. 'Not if *one* of the parents doesn't want him in their life.'

Lucy swayed in her seat as her face blanched to a waxy alabaster.

He moved quickly, instinctively pulling out her chair and pushing her head between her knees. 'Take deep breaths.'

A slither of guilt caught him under his ribs that he'd yelled at her and had caused this, but common sense won over. Lucy wasn't a timid or frail woman and it wasn't the 1800s where tight corsets made women faint if they got upset. She was more than capable of standing up for herself and she did it all the time. So what exactly had upset her? That Ignacio didn't have contact with his mother?

He thought about what had been said just before she'd almost fainted. *Contact with both his parents.* Lucy wasn't a child of divorce. She'd grown up in a stable family with both of her parents. None of it was making much sense.

'Marco.' Her voice was muffled by her lap. 'Let me sit up.'

His hand fell from her silky hair, immediately

missing the softness on his palm, and she sat up slowly. He handed her a glass of water. 'Are you dizzy?'

'No.' She gave herself a small shake. 'I'll be fine. Obviously a long day's caught up with me.'

He supposed that could be true. 'I will drive you home.'

She shook her head. 'Thanks for the offer but that would mean in the morning I'm stuck at Haven without my car.'

'No problem. William can drive you in. He'd be happy to do it.'

Her mouth thinned. 'He would but I'm not going to ask him.'

And there it was again. This issue with William. 'Your father's a good man, Lucy. I think it is sad that you're not closer.'

She stood up with a jerk and pulled her jacket off the back of the chair. 'I think it's sad you're divorced but that doesn't change the situation, does it?'

She had him there. 'True, but with blood relatives things are different. There is a special bond that is worth keeping.'

'I wouldn't know about that,' she muttered. 'I'll see you at Haven.

She walked out the door without a backward glance and despite all his promises to himself he found himself wanting to know what made her tick.

Lucy pulled into the empty clinic car park at six p.m. It had been her day to do the 'rural loop' and she'd enjoyed the long drive and the solitude, although the number of times that thoughts of Marco had intruded, she'd hardly been alone. Yesterday's bombshell of his divorce kept coming back to her as did his words about Ignacio's mother.

She hated how profoundly it had affected her. Hell, she never fainted, but his words had rammed home all the uncertainties about her own life. She'd been waiting months for a phone call, hoping it would solve everything by telling her who she really was and where she belonged. She craved to feel settled and secure again rather than having this constant feeling that gnawed away at her, making her feel hollow. She was living in the detritus of a massive lie and everything she'd ever believed in had vanished. All she wanted was some facts so she could rebuild her life on them.

After gathering up her gear, she walked into the building just as Sue was closing up. 'Hey, Sue.'

'Lucy.' The practice nurse gave her a curt nod as she pressed 'cancel' on the security system. 'I'll leave you to lock up, but before you do, there's a stack of results on your desk that need your signature. I've put the concerning ones on the top including Nyanath Gil's pap test result. I'd appreciate it if you called her tonight.'

'Will do.' Lucy smiled in an attempt to get Sue to thaw but the woman's mouth stayed in a firm line. It was the first time they'd been totally alone since she'd arrived and there were some things she needed to say to Sue, overdue things, despite the waves of animosity that were rolling off her.

Lucy sucked in a fortifying breath. 'William says you took great care of him over the last few weeks and I really appreciate it. Thank you.'

Sue's eyes flashed. 'Someone had to do it.'

She swallowed the hit, telling herself that no one on the outside ever knew the full story of what went on inside a family. Hell, she was *in* the family and she'd had no clue. 'I wasn't here earlier because he didn't tell me.'

Sue folded her arms across her chest. 'Did you ask?'

Ouch! She wanted to yell, *All of this is William's fault not mine,* but there was no point so she fell back on country pleasantries. 'Enjoy your evening, Sue, and please pass on my best wishes to George, Chloe and Liam.'

Sue's mouth lost its tart line. 'Chloe's pregnant. She and Liam decided there was no point in waiting and the baby's due next month.'

'That's lovely news, Sue.' Lucy was genuinely pleased although oddly a tiny part of her ached and she didn't know why. It wasn't like she wanted to marry a sheep farmer like Chloe had, and being a mother should be the last thing on her mind given she had so many unanswered questions about her own life.

Feeling oddly discomfited by the unexpected sensations, she said, 'Goodnight,' and walked down the corridor to William's office.

Working her way through the pathology reports, she made a few phone calls leaving Nyanath to last because she knew her conversation with the Sudanese woman would take a long time. It was never easy trying to explain the need for a repeat pap test due to pre-cancerous cells and yet allay anxiety that it wasn't actually cancer. People always jumped to the worst conclusions first. When she'd hung up the phone, she absently flicked through the mail stack, pulling the medical journals and any mail specifically for William. At the very bottom was a packet addressed to her in Jess's bold script.

Her mouth dried and she picked up the envelope, turning it over slowly. She hadn't spoken to Jess since she'd found out about her and Daniel. Running a paperknife across the seam, she tipped the envelope upside down and half a dozen letters fell out along with an accompanying note from Jess.

Luce, I'm soooo sorry I hurt you. I honestly never meant to, but this thing with Dan, it was bigger than both of us, you know, and it just was always there. I know things weren't great between you, and I should have waited until it was over. What I did was so wrong and I regret it and if I could turn back time I would. Can you ever forgive me? Jess x

Did an apology for sleeping with a friend's boyfriend make any difference to the feelings of betrayal, even though the relationship was floundering? Could a friendship ever survive something like that?

She conceded the fact that Jess had admitted fault did help a little bit, and she knew in her heart that she and Daniel had been all but over but everything was still too raw for her to begin repairing the friendship just yet. Her shaky fingers sorted the envelopes and she recognised her bank statement, her health insurance renewal and a newsletter from her favourite shoe shop. There was only one real letter and it was in a small envelope. It was addressed to her by hand with no return address and it had been franked in Sydney.

She slid William's silver paperknife carefully through the top of the envelope and pulled out a piece of blue-lined paper. It was covered in neat writing.

Dear Lucy—Jade as I've always thought of you.

Her fingers trembled. This was the contact she'd waited so long for. She'd expected a phone call, but she didn't care that it was a letter. It was contact. From her birth mother. The urge to rush through the letter—to find the part where her mother wanted to meet her—was so strong that she made herself read it out loud to slow herself down.

'I got your letter. You're a doctor. That's an achievement that can never be taken away from you. I clean houses which isn't quite as important but I get satisfaction from closing the door on a house that is neat, clean and tidy and at peace for a moment.'

Lucy smiled. She'd always enjoyed the feeling of a tidy room and a neat workspace.

'I'm married now with two teenage sons and my life is finally settled after years of uncertainty. I've found a form of happiness that I never thought I could.'

Happiness flooded her. She had brothers! After all these years she had an instant family and the siblings she'd longed for.

'Getting your letter was a shock and it's taken me this long to face answering it because it sucked me back twenty-six years to a bad place for me. Part of me always wondered if you'd make contact and when you were a teenager I sort of expected it. When I didn't hear from you then I finally let you go. I needed to let you go. I gave you up because at sixteen I couldn't be the mother you needed. Nothing has changed.'

Lucy's throat tightened so much she stopped reading out loud because she couldn't form words. Frantically, her eyes scanned the next paragraph.

I've never told my husband or my children about you and I never will. It's taken me a long time to find some peace in my life and I can't risk losing it. Not now. I'm so sorry your mother passed away but you have your father and your life as a doctor. Please respect my wishes and don't try and contact me again.
Allison

Lucy could barely breathe as she re-read the last paragraph, hoping against hope that she'd read the words wrong.

Don't try and contact me again.

Hot tears scalded her cheeks as her long-held hopes of the last six months shattered into painful shards with jagged edges. She bled eviscerating pain and her hands shook so much that the letter fluttered to the desk. Everything she'd spent six months hoping for had just turned to dust.

Her mother didn't want her.

Had never wanted her.

Her breaths came in short, jerky bursts and her brain was stuck on a repetitive track of, *She doesn't want me.* She put her hands over her ears but it didn't stop the voice in her head. An overwhelming need to flee swamped her and she stood up fast, sending the office chair skating back across the room. Plucking her bag from the floor, she ran down the corridor and with numb fingers somehow managed the complicated locking up process. Through a veil of tears, she got into her car, started the ignition, threw it into gear and drove. When she reached the main road she knew she couldn't go to Haven. She couldn't face William this upset or hear him say, 'I told you so.'

She pulled the steering wheel to the left, taking the opposite direction but without a clue where to go. There wasn't anyone in Bulla Creek she could confide in because no one knew the secret that the Pattersons had held so close for so long. Despite her anger with William and Ruth over everything that had happened, she didn't want their story to be the butt of gossiping groups. She turned a corner and another, driving aimlessly until she found herself outside a familiar house and the one person she could face talking to. The one person who might just understand.

She let her head fall onto the steering wheel and wept.

Marco couldn't settle. He'd been looking forward to having an evening to himself as Ignacio, having had so much fun with William the night before, had invited himself to Haven for a 'real sleep over'. William had been enthusiastic about the idea, Ignacio was very excited, and because it was Friday night, Marco had agreed. Right now he should be kicking back on the couch and reading the novel he hadn't had time to pick up for weeks, but unwisely he'd checked his emails prior to sitting down. That had blown apart all his plans of relaxing.

In disbelief, he'd printed out the offending email, hoping that reading it in hard copy would somehow change the words.

Dear Dr Rodriguez,
As per the Migration Act of 1994, if you or a member of your family has a condition where the provision of health care or community services would be likely to result in a *significant* cost to the Australian community, then the visa application is rejected. Your son Ignacio Rodriguez's condition of cerebral palsy fails to meet the health requirement and permanent residency is denied.
Your temporary 457 Visa is valid for 180 days.

Incandescent with rage, he balled the paper and threw it across the room. This privileged country, so desperate for doctors to work in far flung places, had fallen over itself to have him come and work in the outback. Now, when he wanted to stay and commit to this community, spend his life and his money here, they rejected his son and in doing so denied Bulla Creek the second doctor it so badly needed.

His fury dimmed slightly as fatigue clawed at

him. It wasn't physical tiredness, though, but an emotional weariness that was now as much a part of him as his curly hair. From the moment Ignacio had been born and had looked up at him with his bright eyes, Marco had been fighting for him. At first it was fighting for his mother's love and he'd failed miserably so now he was mother and father. He'd had more success with access to therapy but none of it had come without diligence and constancy of effort.

His most recent battle had been to get an aide at school so his physical limitations didn't impede his learning. He fought to create opportunities so Ignacio had the same chances to excel academically as his able-bodied peers and he fought prejudices all the time. *Dios,* he would fight this visa ruling too.

First he needed a drink. Then he needed a lawyer who was an expert in immigration law. As he crossed the living room on his way to the kitchen, his front doorbell pealed incessantly. The two previous times this had happened he'd opened the door to find someone in urgent need of a doctor. 'You see!' He shook his fist in the air as if the bureaucrat who'd ruled against him could see and hear him. 'This town needs me.'

Grabbing his medical bag, he opened the door. 'How can I help—? *Querido Dios*. Lucy?' Shocked, he stood perfectly still, staring at her. Then fear tore through his heart. 'What's happened? Is it Ignacio? William?'

She rushed past him into the house and then hesitated for a moment as if she wasn't sure why she was there. She raised her face to his and looked at him from blank eyes in a red and blotchy face. 'I… They're fine, I think, I…' Her shoulders sagged and her body seemed to crumple. 'It's me.'

The pain in her voice lanced him, pushing his own concerns sideways. Instinctively, he held out his arms, wanting to protect and shelter her from whatever it was that was distressing her so much.

She stepped straight into them, pressing her head onto his chest and resting it under his shoulder. Her body shuddered, racked with sobs that seemed to come up all the way from her soul.

He gently held her apart from him and stared down into her traumatised face. 'What's wrong? Tell me.'

But she couldn't form any words so he let her rest back against him, stroking her hair and waiting until she was calmer. He dropped his head close to hers, breathing in the vanilla scent of her shampoo, and his body stirred.

He swallowed hard, hating it that he was aroused when he should be concentrating on giving her comfort. *'Está bien.* It's okay, you are safe here.'

Slowly, her breathing steadied and her fingers which had clamped around the front of his shirt relaxed. She looked up at him, her eyes the colour of snow-filled clouds made even more luminous from the tears. 'I'm sorry. I've made your shirt all wet.'

'No problem.' The huskiness in his voice betrayed him totally. Every part of him roared to kiss her.

Comfort only. Treat her as you would a child.

He pulled a handkerchief from his pocket and dabbed at the wet trail of tears that snaked down her cheeks, and then he wiped her nose.

She hiccoughed. 'You've done this before.'

'I am a father and used to tears.'

'Yours or Ignacio's?'

He slowly stroked some damp strands of hair behind her ear and thought about his battles for his son in the past and the fights that were still to come. 'Sometimes both.'

She kept her gaze fixed on his and raised her hand to his cheek. 'God, life can totally suck.'

'*Sí*, it can.' Her heat burned into him and he wanted to forget everything—the unfairness of life, the promises he'd made to himself—and just bend his head, capture her lips and lose himself in her hot, lush mouth.

She sighed. 'How do you deal with it?'

'One day at a time.'

'Right now, I'm down to one hour at a time.' Rising on her toes, she slid her hand into his hair and with her fingers pressing into his scalp she pulled his face down to hers and kissed him.

Her wet lips met his dry ones, firing desperate and frantic need into his blood, which instantly became part of him.

One hour at a time.

He knew exactly what she meant. Life could change in a heartbeat. He had no clue what had sent her here so distraught, but he knew he needed her now as much as she needed him. They were using each other to forget but he didn't need regrets. Her regrets.

With superhuman effort he broke the kiss, his breath coming fast. 'Are you sure?'

'That I want to have sex with you right now?'

'Yes.'

Shadows scudded through her eyes. 'Do you want to have sex with me right now?'

'*Dios,* yes, but—'

'It's just sex, Marco.' Her smile said, *Don't panic. I'm not moving in.* 'We're just two people giving in to the lust that's been pulling at us from the moment we met. Don't overthink it. Accept it. No past, no future, just now.'

Just now. He'd wanted her for days. *No past, no future.* God help him, after that email he wanted her more than ever, if only to give temporary ease to his permanent heartache.

Marco's lips captured Lucy's with a force so strong it sent days of restrained passion tearing through her so fast she forgot to breathe. His arms pulled her off her feet, holding her tightly, and her body instantly melded against his—grateful and seeking. He felt solid, hard and hot, but most importantly, he wanted her.

Right now she needed to be wanted and needed to feel safe—needed it badly.

He broke the kiss for breath. 'Bed.'

'Really?' She eyed the generous sized couch. She didn't want to slow things down in case he changed his mind so she started walking backwards toward it while she undid the buttons on his shirt. Her fingertips brushed the smooth skin of his chest, skin she knew hid toned and tight muscles.

His large hand closed over hers, trapping her fingers. 'Really.' His index finger trailed down her cheek and his dark eyes shimmered as they hooked hers. 'I do my best work in bed. I assume you want my best work?'

Her legs lost all power to hold her up.

As he held her steady, his laugh said it all and then he kissed her again, this time his tongue flicking into her mouth in a tantalising display of what was to come.

They ran to the bedroom.

As she kicked off her shoes, she took in the made bed and general tidiness. 'You're neat.'

'I have a cleaning woman who comes on

Fridays.' He pulled off his shirt, letting it fall to the floor.

She watched mesmerised as sinew and muscles and tendons worked together in one fluid and rippling motion. 'You're absolutely stunning.'

'I think I am supposed to say that to you.'

She shrugged. 'I get told I'm more cute and wholesome than gorgeous.'

He stepped in close, his hands easing her sundress over her head until she stood before him in a black and white lace demi-bra with matching bikini briefs. She'd always loved shoes *and* underwear. His gaze burned a trail of longing through her as it flicked across the lace line of her left breast before dipping at her décolletage and rising again.

He lowered his head until his lips brushed her ear and when he spoke his voice was raspy and low. 'Cute and wholesome does not wear underwear like this.'

A shiver of delight tingled between her legs and she pressed her hand flat over his nipple. Remembering the moment in the corridor at the hospital, she caressed it with her thumb. 'I want to explore every inch of your body.'

This time he shuddered and it rolled off him and directly into her. She closed her mouth around his other nipple. His guttural groan vibrated into her mouth and the next minute her feet were off the floor, her back was pressed into the mattress and she was staring up into dark chocolate eyes alight with heady need.

She grinned and traced the dark hair on his belly that arrowed down toward his waistband. 'So, this best work of yours…'

He caught her hands with his, pinning them lightly by her sides. 'It happens when you let me pleasure you.'

His voice caressed her like the touch of a feather, but when his mouth closed over the lace of her bra, suckling her through the flimsy material, pure pleasure poured through her. Her body immediately begged for so much more. 'Take my bra off.'

'Shh.' He shook his head. 'I do my best work without instructions.'

'In that case, I'll stop talk—'

He swallowed her words with his kiss, and she gave herself over to the wondrous pressure of his mouth on hers, and the explorations of his hands as they skimmed over her thighs. His fingers moved tantalisingly slowly from thigh to hip to waist—a pleasure pathway that built on the desire that had simmered inside her for days and days, until she thought she'd combust from joy.

With an expert flick, he unclasped her bra and her breasts tumbled from their flimsy, lacy prison. She hugged his sigh of delight to herself.

With an almost reverent touch, he traced ever-decreasing circles on her soft flesh until her nipples stood tall—seeking and aching for his touch. Then his tongue licked their base and she heard herself moan.

'If you like that, *mi amor*, perhaps you will enjoy this.' He ran his teeth across the tip of her nipple before taking her into his mouth.

Jagged sensations of agony and ecstasy whipped through her until deep down inside her everything throbbed and called out for more. Her head thrashed against the pillow as her hands plunged into his hair. Oh, God, she never wanted him to stop. He trailed his mouth down her belly—kissing, licking and branding her, whipping her body into a frenzy of craving that was ramped up notch by notch with every addictive touch. Caresses that gave so much and yet always taunted that there might be more.

His mouth reached her panties and while he pressed kisses along the line of elastic, his fingers toyed with the edges of her crotch. Sometimes they stroked the material, sometimes they flicked underneath to touch her. She was wet, slick and throbbing and her muscles screamed to close around him.

In an agony of unending pleasure, she writhed, pushing against his hand, desperate for the pressure of his palm cupping her. Nothing existed except this feeling of bliss and her urge for it to carry her along with it. His thumb brushed her clitoris and she cried out his name. Then his finger slid inside her and she shattered instantly, drowning in liquid pleasure.

He rolled away from her and as cool air rushed over her she heard the slide of a bedside drawer. Her hand shot out, closing tightly around his forearm.

'I am not leaving, Lucy.'

She gasped and dropped her hand. It was like he was inside her head, reading her thoughts and seeing through all her protective layers right down to her bruised and abandoned heart. She forced out a laugh. 'Of course you're not. Especially when I'm about to give you the best sex you've ever had.'

'Is that a promise?' He quickly shucked his pants and put on a condom. Now he sat back on his haunches, his hands resting gently on her ankles and his erection tall and proud.

She gazed at him in his full glory of manhood and a tiny concern that she wouldn't quite match up taunted her. She lifted her arms above her head, knowing that her breasts would rise. 'Absolutely.'

With a raw groan, he pulled her up until they were at eye-level. She linked her arms around his neck, wrapped her legs around his waist, and let his hands knead her buttocks.

He kissed her slowly and deeply as he raised her up.

Kissing him back, she lowered herself down onto him, her body ripe and ready to accept him, instantly moulding around his strength as if he'd been designed for her. With a cry of delight, she gave in to the power of the beat, tuning into the rhythm of life and she let it take them higher and higher until they spun out together, soaring high above themselves and where for a precious moment time stood still and all earthly ties fell away. Nothing existed but the bliss.

Then, spent, they fell back on the bed.

CHAPTER EIGHT

MARCO fired up the barbeque, turning it up high so the grill would be the perfect temperature to sear the meat. He couldn't remember the last time he'd felt quite this relaxed and loose-limbed, but he had no desire to examine the feeling too closely. He just…was. He turned at the sound of heels on the deck and smiled.

Lucy's hair was still damp from the shower and instead of falling in its usual smooth wave, the strands clumped together. She gave him a wide smile, one he knew she always used when she was nervous or wanted something. 'Thanks for the shower.'

'Are you hungry?'

She blushed and then laughed at herself. 'After that work-out, I think we both deserve to be.'

He grinned and dropped a kiss on her nose. 'So that is a "yes"?'

Her expression sobered. 'Please don't think you

have to feed me, Marco. I'm happy to leave now and next time I see you we'll be back to being Dr Patterson and Dr Rodriguez.'

It was a gift he should take but as he stared down at the scoop neck of her top, taking in the curve of creamy-white skin that he knew ended up around rose-bud pink nipples, he didn't want her to leave. Not just yet. 'Stay for a glass of wine and I'll cook you a steak. If you go now, Ignacio will expect you to play his new favourite game that William taught him.'

'Go Fish.' Her voice sounded flat and weary.

'*Sí*, you know it?'

'It was the first game I remember William teaching me.' Her throat convulsed and she quickly poured herself a glass of wine, sculling the contents in two long gulps.

'And it drove you to drink?' He'd meant it as a joke but he saw familiar shadows scudding across her eyes and given the state she'd been in when she'd arrived earlier, it was time to pry.

She set down the glass. 'I think I should just leave.'

He shook his head. 'Stay. You just drank a glass of wine on an empty stomach so you cannot drive.' He stroked her cheek. 'Lucy, your father is a generous and good man who clearly loves you. Why does a happy childhood memory have you guzzling merlot?'

She bit her lip. 'Because—' her voice was so soft he had to strain to hear '—William isn't my father.'

He frowned thinking he must have misheard her. *'Qué?'*

'Exactly.' She poured two glasses of wine and handed him one before sitting down. 'Try magnifying your surprise a million times and you still won't come close to how I felt when I found out that after twenty-six years the man I idolised wasn't my father. How it stuns me still.'

'I can't even imagine.' As much as he felt for Lucy's sense of betrayal, he now understood the sadness that ringed William. 'When did you find out?'

'Earlier this year. Not long after the woman I'd always thought was my mother died.'

He picked up her hand, cradling it in his. 'William's wife? Ruth?'

'Yes. Neither of them are my biological parents.' She took a small sip of wine. 'When I was a little girl I used to watch Ruth sitting at her dressing table putting on her jewellery before she and—before they went out to the Bulla Creek races, or the polo matches and the community dances. I loved a particular pair of her earrings she always wore to parties and each time she put them on I'd say to her, "When can I wear those?" She'd always say, "The day my feet stop dancing."'

Lucy closed her eyes for a moment before blowing out a long breath. 'When she died so unexpectedly, I was bereft and I thought that if I wore the earrings I'd always have a part of her with me. After the funeral I asked William about them and he told me to take them back to Perth with me so I went into their bedroom to get them. She'd always kept them in a box in the small drawer next to the mirror, but when I looked they weren't there. So I started clearing things out, hoping to find them, only I found a lot more than earrings.' Her knuckles whitened on the stem of the wineglass. 'My adoption papers were at the very back of the drawer.'

He held her close and pressed a kiss into her

damp hair, trying to absorb some of her pain. 'And you'd never suspected?'

'I didn't have a clue. Maybe it was because I didn't have any siblings to feel different from, I don't know. But suddenly everything I understood about my life was false and I'd lost my history. I wasn't me and my life was a lie. I was so angry.' She stood up abruptly and threw the steaks onto the grill, watching the flare of the flames searing the meat. 'I'm still angry. How could they hide the truth from me?'

That was a question he could answer. 'Because they love you.'

Lucy couldn't believe her ears and she spun around to face him. The night she'd found out, the *only* thing William could say to her was, 'We love you so much.'

She fought the tightness in her chest. 'You sound just like William and it's a cop-out, not a reason.'

He opened his hands. 'I am not saying it was the right thing to do but they probably thought they were protecting you.'

She hugged herself to try and stop the surge of emotions that always took her back to that dark, dark moment when she'd opened up the yellowed pages to see the word 'adopted'. She didn't want to keep going back there because it always left her so drained and worn out. 'Believe me, the only people they were protecting were themselves.'

He stood up and walked over to her, resting his hand gently on her shoulder, and gazed down at her with a knowing look. 'I know it's hard but when you're a parent yourself, perhaps you'll understand.'

'Don't patronise me.' She shrugged away his touch, not even able to visualise herself as a mother.

His eyes darkened. 'I am not patronising you but when you hold your baby in your arms there is such a surge of love and protection that it changes you.'

She started shaking. 'I don't believe that for a moment. You told me that your ex-wife didn't want to be part of Ignacio's life and my—' She swallowed, trying to keep calm, but her chest cramped and her throat tightened. 'My birth mother gave me away and now she has the chance to know me as an adult, she writes and says she doesn't want me.'

He scooped her in close, cradling her like a child. 'Some women are not meant to be mothers. Bianca is one and perhaps your birth mother is another.'

She shook her head. 'She was sixteen and I understand at that age, back then, perhaps she couldn't keep me but now she's a mother of two boys. My half-brothers.' She heard her voice rising and she wiped her face with the back of her hand. 'She doesn't want them to know about me. I'm just a dirty secret from her past that she wants to forget.'

'No. You are never that.' He tilted her chin. 'You are a talented doctor and a beautiful woman with a shoe addiction.'

She mustered up a watery smile, appreciating his kindness, but it didn't stop the voice deep inside her from repeating what it had been saying for months. *You have no clue who you are.* 'You forgot the decadent underwear.'

His dark eyes shimmered. 'That I will never forget.' Still holding her hand, he flipped the steaks. 'Biology is just a starting point, Lucy.'

As ridiculous as she knew it was, her heart ached for what she'd never known and the person she might have been if her biological parents had raised her. 'Is that what you're going to tell Ignacio when he asks about his mother?'

He dropped her hand and picked up a plate. 'I will tell him that his mother is the one who missed out on the joy of knowing him.'

She drank more wine. 'He'll still feel empty.'

'I know.' Marco pulled the steaks off the grill with a sigh. 'And it's my fault.'

She sat back down at the table confused. 'How do you figure that exactly?'

He put the succulent steak down in front of her and passed the salad before sitting down. She watched him fork lettuce onto his plate, slice off a piece of meat and chew it slowly, letting the silence ride.

Finally, he met her gaze. 'I had always wanted children so when Bianca told me she was pregnant three years earlier than we planned, I was thrilled. Bianca was not. She is a perfectionist and she saw the pregnancy as slowing down her career. She wanted to have a termination. I convinced her not to because I believed the regrets we'd both have if she did would ruin our marriage.'

He bit into another piece of meat, chewing with a tight jaw. 'I think our relationship was beyond repair then but I didn't recognise it.'

Lucy thought of Daniel. 'There are times in our life when we need to believe things are better than they really are and relationship-blindness can serve a purpose.'

He raised a brow. 'This boyfriend you just broke up with?'

'He broke up with me, actually.' She rubbed her temples. 'I should have seen it coming but I didn't want to open my eyes or my mind to the possibility because I needed him as an anchor. My mother had just died, only she wasn't my mother, and my father was no longer my father and I had no clue if I was coming or going. As it turned out, he wasn't anchor material and I probably shouldn't have expected him to be.'

'I am sorry to hear that.' He linked his fingers with hers and gave her a half-smile. 'You are right, I needed that blindness. I was going to be a father and I needed to believe it would all work out. Bianca had no interest in the pregnancy and

I found myself defending her behaviour to my family. They were horrified that I had chosen all the nursery furniture and purchased all the baby clothes. So many times I heard myself saying, "Bianca is too tired, too busy, too…"'

Lucy watched his richly tanned fingers against her whiter hand and waited. The outcome was known but she wanted to hear how it had played out. She rationalised her fascination with Marco, telling herself that by knowing she could perhaps understand his almost self-contained relationship with his son.

And then what? Help? You need to sort out your own life first.

Marco let out a long sigh. 'Ignacio was born eight weeks premature and Bianca returned to work at the hospital when he was seven days old. I thought it was her way of coping and a way to be near the baby. I visited him in the nursery three to four times a day but I never saw her there. When I arranged to meet her to share a feeding time, she would often be late.'

'Did you know about his CP then?'

He shook his head. 'We thought he was a just a premature baby with normal delay and that by his first birthday he would have caught up. We brought him home when he was term plus two weeks but not a lot changed with Bianca. She was always at work and I didn't question her long hours because I knew Ignacio's arrival had come at a bad time for her career plans. I wanted to support her but I also knew her baby needed her.'

She wondered about post-natal depression. 'It sounds tough.'

He shrugged. 'Between me, my mother and a nanny, we got through each day. I don't remember much of it. I was worried about Bianca, worried about Ignacio and I was living in a fog of exhaustion...' His eyes clouded as if he was back in the past.

She finally prompted him. 'Until?'

He grimaced. 'When Ignacio was nine months old, we got the official diagnosis of cerebral palsy. It sounds strange but I was relieved that we finally knew what I had suspected for months. Now we could plan and get the help Ignacio needed. Bianca refused to discuss anything with the doctor and when we got home from the paediatrician's office, she packed a bag and said she was leaving. She told me she'd never wanted a child and she did not want one that was damaged.' His voice turned harsh. 'I am *never* telling Ignacio those words.'

Her delicious meal turned to stone in her stomach not just because a mother had rejected her child but because she knew exactly what that was like. 'You won't ever have to tell him. He's an intelligent boy and he'll work it out all by himself.'

Marco's fist hit the table, making the plates rattle. 'He is surrounded by love and that is what is important. The people who raise you, walk the floors at night patting your back, march you out of underage parties and stay up late helping with homework, they are the parents. I always tell Ignacio that I love him. His grandparents love him and they will arrive here soon, and William loves him. Just like William loves you. You need to accept his love.'

She pushed her plate away. 'It's not that straightforward, Marco.'

'It can be. You came back to see him.'

'I came back because he was sick and I'm not totally heartless. Don't read more into it than that.'

She gazed at his handsome face and knew he

didn't really understand. How could he? He could look around his family and see who he inherited his curly hair from, recognise his mannerisms in his parents and brothers, and share a blood bond that she never could. Suddenly she felt unbelievably tired. 'I should go.' She stood up and the world swayed. She sat down again. 'Sorry, I think I need you to drive me back to Haven.'

'I have had as much wine as you. Neither of us is going anywhere.'

She dropped her head into her hands. 'Oh, God, this is embarrassing.'

He laughed, his eyes dancing with fun as he stroked her hair. 'I have a guest room and it will not take long to make up the bed.'

Part of her wanted to call his bluff and spend the night in the guest room but her traitorous body leapt into life at his touch. 'I wouldn't want to put you to any trouble.'

He leaned in, his lips brushing her ear. 'You are a very obliging guest.'

Tingling need made her voice breathy. 'That's me. I'll do anything to help. All you just have to ask.'

He whispered his detailed request into her ear.

With her body alight with heady desire she pulled him into her arms and did exactly as he'd asked.

'Marco's coming over,' William announced a moment after his phone pinged with an incoming text.

It was Sunday night and a familiar shot of excitement pulsed through Lucy. Thankfully William was still looking down at his phone and she had a moment to suck in some deep breaths and cool her cheeks. She hadn't seen Marco since very early Saturday morning, but every time she thought of him her body tingled with a craving that both thrilled and worried her. Sex with Marco was supposed to get him out of her system, not inculcate him.

She turned the page of the weekend magazine she'd been reading, hoping to look casual and only moderately interested. 'Does he usually just pop in?'

William frowned. 'He and Ignacio often drop by but he never usually texts me to announce it. I can't imagine why he's coming this late in the day.'

The click of the back gate and the crunch of gravel had Lucy up and on her feet. 'We're about to find out.'

Marco opened the door, his face lined with strain which was in stark contrast to the last time she'd seen him in his bed and given him a deep kiss goodbye.

'Hey, buddy.' William's face lit up when Iggie entered the room. Using his walking stick, he did a complicated hockey-stick-like cross against one of Ignacio's crutches.

Laughing, the boy returned the action as if it was a secret handshake between the two of them and a lump formed in Lucy's throat. Growing up, she and William always had in-jokes and secrets, so much so that Ruth had often joked, 'Just as well I know you love me because you're such a daddy's girl.'

But she wasn't daddy's girl any more. All that closeness had imploded, leaving her empty and adrift.

You miss it.

She bit her lip against her permanent heartache and then her protective anger rose again. *His* lie had stolen their relationship and there was no going back. Now when she looked at William, all she could do was wonder who her biological father was and lament that she'd never know.

'Are you okay?' Marco asked quietly, his eyes far too perceptive.

She tossed her head and concentrated on the here and now. 'Fine. Are you and Iggie staying for dinner?'

'That's a good idea, Lucy.' William limped towards Marco with his hand extended.

'I don't want to impose, but I do need to speak with you privately.'

William looked thoughtful. 'If it's about the practice, Lucy should hear it too. We can do it over a meal.'

Marco tilted his head toward Ignacio and Lucy realised that whatever Marco wanted to talk about he didn't want his son to hear.

'Iggie, do you want to watch some TV?' Lucy asked. 'It's going to be more fun than listening to us talk about work.'

The little boy looked at his father who nodded his approval. 'Yes, please.'

Lucy set Iggie up in the den with a drink, some chips and the children's channel, and came back into the room to hear William saying, 'That's outrageous.'

'What is?' Lucy joined both men at the table.

Marco's hands fisted tightly. 'I have been denied permanent residency because Ignacio failed the health test. He is considered a risk to the public purse.'

His pain sliced into her heart and without thinking she laid her hand over the top of his. 'That's just wrong.'

William shot her a look that combined surprise and a tiny flash of hope. 'In six months Bulla Creek might be back to one doctor and it needs two.'

She shook her head slowly against his veiled request. She wasn't ever returning to live in Bulla Creek. Looking back at Marco, she said, 'We have to fight this.'

This time Marco shook his head. '*I* have to fight this. It is my battle.'

With a jolt, she realised from the moment Ignacio had been born, Marco had been fighting for him on his own. That wasn't how things happened in Bulla Creek. 'No, it isn't just your battle. Hell, the government needed you enough to bring you here. Iggie's settled and goes to the local school, he's integrated and bright and we have to prove to the faceless bean-counters that they're wrong. You came here to start a new life, you want to be here and the town needs you. It's their fight too.' She squeezed her fingers around his fist as she leaned forward. 'What can we do?'

'We're here to support you and Ignacio in any way we can, Marco,' William said.

Marco felt William and Lucy's gazes boring into him, waiting for him to tell them what he needed. It set up the strangest sensation in his chest—a pull of belonging and the equal push of his own rejection. *Dios*, he'd got so used to doing things on his own because that way he could control his life. Protect Ignacio's. How was this battle different?

Only he knew it was because the lawyer hadn't sounded very positive. Could he ask for help?

He was struck by the irony that in Lucy's offer to help, she'd unintentionally agreed to work with William. His visa problem was a common bond for them, a connection, which was something they needed badly if they were ever to close the massive fissure in their relationship. He wanted that for both of them. Lucy's grey eyes were fixed on him, filled with empathy and the light of indignation born from injustice. Something inside him softened. 'I spent yesterday on the phone to a lawyer and—'

'But yesterday was Saturday. When did you hear from the department of immigration?'

Marco could see her mind connecting the dots. 'Friday evening.'

She blinked. Twice. A wry smile wove across her lips as understanding dawned in her eyes. They'd both had a reason to reach out to each other that night.

'The day is irrelevant, Lucy,' William said, getting the conversation back on track with his usual sharp-minded style. 'What did the lawyer say?'

Marco ran his hand through his hair. 'He is going to lodge an appeal but it could take months.'

'You need more than an appeal. We need some noisy rural outrage.' Lucy jumped up, opened a drawer in the large dresser and pulled out a notepad. 'William, do you know anyone in the media?'

'No.'

'Oh.' She sat down drumming her pen against the paper. 'What about you, Marco?'

'I spoke to a reporter once after I delivered a baby in a motor home.'

'Do you remember who he was or where he worked?' Lucy's expression urged him to think and think hard.

He recalled the reporter with her blonde-streaked hair and immaculate nails urging him to accept her business card, and saying that if he was ever in Perth he should call her for a drink. He wasn't fool enough to tell Lucy that. 'I think her business card is somewhere in my office.'

'It's a start.' She jotted it down on the pad.

'Bulla Creek is hosting the polo the weekend after next,' William added.

Lucy frowned. 'So?'

William smiled. 'The Perth press always attends because the sponsor hosts a generous marquee where the drinks flow. Occasionally a politician attends.'

The permanent tension that ringed Lucy whenever she was with her father relaxed slightly and she gave him a genuine smile—the first one Marco had ever seen her give him. 'I think you're onto something, William.' Her attention shot back to Marco. 'Can you ride a horse?'

He was momentarily affronted. 'What sort of a question is that to ask an Argentine? I grew up on a polo horse.'

'Sensational.' Her eyes sparkled at him. 'You'll be picture-perfect on a horse and a media darling. Oh, do you have a horse?'

William laughed. 'David Henderson was so desperate to have Marco join the polo club, he offered him the use of one of his ponies until Marco bought his own.'

Stunned surprise flitted across her face. 'Wow, you must be good. David Henderson's very fussy about his horses.' Her looping writing started to cover the page. 'For this to work we need a town meeting. I can organise that and we'll prime everyone so no matter who talks to the press the message will be the same. I can get a—'

'You do realise, Lucy, if you get involved in this you need to extend your time in Bulla Creek,' William said quietly, hope lining his face.

Lucy's mouth tightened as her father's words sank in. Maybe this was what she needed—a chance to heal the wounds of the past.

Marco saw a glimmer of hope and immediately justified his idea, telling himself he was doing this to help Lucy and William. The more time the two of them spent together, the more chance they had to work through the hard emotions. Of course that meant they had to start talking and so far he hadn't seen any evidence of that. Asking Lucy to stay was all about her and William and nothing to do with keeping her in his bed a little bit longer.

Under the table and safely out of William's sight, he ran his foot along the back of her leg. 'If you can find the time to stay...'

Her eyes widened at the unspoken suggestion and she stared straight at him, her grey eyes flickering with desire. She licked her lips. 'I...' She didn't look at her father. 'I suppose I can delay moving house another week.'

William grunted, '"Outback Australians deserve health care." Write it down, Lucy. "Bulla Creek deserves to have its dedicated and well-respected doctor remain in Australia, living in the community he values and loves."'

Marco glimpsed a spark of the old William. Was that a good sign?

Lucy chewed her pen. 'That's pretty good, but if we add in...'

Marco listened intently as Lucy and William batted ideas around, extending thoughts, tweaking them and using their years of local knowledge and their understanding of politics to create a first draft of a press release.

He let their energy and enthusiasm envelop him and felt a tiny release in some of the anxiety that had been spinning inside him from the moment he'd read the email. A small seed of hope sprouted that this plan to get some media coverage might just work. If it didn't, at least his problem had put Lucy and William on a shared path.

Lucy's mind was on fire, not just because of the unambiguous desire in Marco's eyes but by the invigorating debate with William. Only she didn't want to think about how good it had felt because she was still so hurt by what he'd done. What Ruth had done and how it had derailed her so badly.

She pulled her mind back from the mess and concentrated on writing down her ideas for how to put some pressure on the department of immigration.

William rose to his feet and rested his hand for a moment on the table as if to steady himself. 'You two start throwing dinner together and I'll make some phone calls now so we make sure we have the district's most influential families at this meeting tomorrow.' He disappeared down the hall.

'Will Ignacio eat cold chicken and salad?' Lucy asked, wondering if he didn't, what else she could offer.

Marco smiled at her. 'He will enjoy that.'

'Great.' She stood up, her stomach doing somersaults from his smile, and she extended her hand. 'Come on then, you're up too.'

Marco grabbed her hand but instead of rising, he pulled her into his lap, pressed his lips to hers and gave her a long and smouldering kiss. A kiss so similar to all his others with its play of heat and need that turned her limbs liquid, and yet so very different with its lingering touch of something that seemed to stretch out between them like a piece of fine wire.

Connecting them in some vague way.

Sex was all you and he agreed to. It's all you can give at the moment.

I know that. I'm not stupid.

And yet the feeling remained.

Shocked and confused, she slid off his lap. 'You know what would be great? If you and Ignacio had your photos taken together.'

He flinched and the familiar shields of protection for Ignacio slotted into place. 'Is it really necessary?'

She chose her words carefully, remembering how he'd reacted at the soccer nets. 'The message will be a lot more powerful with him.'

He stood up but he didn't look convinced. 'He does not need pity.'

'He won't get it.' She rested her hand on his forearm. 'Iggie's a gregarious and delightful child who wins hearts easily. Pictures of the two of you together would be really powerful. Emotion is the best strategy to use to fight this unemotional ruling.'

'I can win this without putting him in the spotlight.'

She linked her arms around his neck wondering if he could win this fight without using every weapon in his arsenal. 'Bulla Creek needs you.'

She closed her ears to the echo of, 'So do I.'

CHAPTER NINE

MARCO stood on the red-dirt cliffs and gazed down onto the white-sand beach and smiled. The colours always astounded him. How did the desert stop so abruptly? It was as if nature had built a barrier that prevented the red sand going any further and insisting the white sand take over. If he shut out the red sand of the dunes, the beach reminded him of the beautiful beaches of Argentina but without the crowds.

A picnic rug and hamper sat on the sand, along with scattered beach toys and a pair of crutches. Lucy and Ignacio sat in the clear, blue-green waters of the Indian Ocean and Ignacio had a bucket and was pouring water over Lucy. She was holding her hands up and laughing and then she wrestled the bucket from him and did the same back.

He laughed, feeling the stress of the day start to ebb away. He'd come to Point Henry to run the weekly clinic, and the previous evening Lucy had said, 'The Bulla Creek clinic is closed tomorrow afternoon. Why don't I pick Iggie up from school and drive him over to the Point? It's only forty minutes and you can do the whole father and son swimming thing. I'll bring a picnic.'

Marco had been worried it would tire his son too much and had said no, but Lucy had countered with the fact it was a pupil-free day the next day and she'd pack his pyjamas so he could sleep on the way home. Then she'd stepped in close and kissed him, her tongue both cajoling and giving all at the same time, and his reservations had slipped away. Later, after she'd once again shared his bed, Marco had suggested she invite William to come to the beach as well. At the time she'd been snuggled up to him with her head on his chest and her hair tickling his nose. Her reply had consisted of 'Hmm' followed by another kiss.

Now as he glanced along the beach he couldn't see any other people so she obviously hadn't taken his suggestion on board. He rubbed his chin, feeling the end of day stubble on his palm, and wondered what it would take to cut through

Lucy's hurt so she realised she was losing too much by freezing William out of her life.

The water looked inviting after a long day at work and with a roar of delight, he ran down the beach and scooped up Ignacio, swinging him around and around over the water. His son's squeals of delight filled him with joy and as he sat down in the shallows with him, something made him look at Lucy.

Her gaze was transfixed on the two of them and yet she seemed to be looking straight through them, her expression both happy and desperately sad all at the same time. Deep down inside him a dull pain throbbed for her. 'Lucy?'

She blinked as if she was returning to him after being somewhere else. 'That looks like awesome fun.'

'*Papá*,' Ignacio panted, still breathless from the game. 'Swing Lucy.'

Lucy laughed. 'I think I'm a bit too heavy for your daddy to do that.'

'Never.' He pulled her to her feet, loving the look and the feel of her in a royal blue bikini, and wishing he could lower her into the water and make love to her. But in front of Ignacio, everything had to be PG rated. Swinging her was the perfect excuse to touch her. 'I can swing you but I need deeper water. Ignacio, you must stay here to watch and not come into the water without me.'

'Okay.'

'*Gracias.*' After Ignacio's recent spate of pushing against Marco's instructions, it was a pleasant surprise to find him so co-operative.

Wrapping his arms around Lucy's bare waist and with her back pressed hard against him, he carried her out a small way and then swung her around and around. Her laughter vibrated through him and he deliberately fell backwards into the water, pulling her with him. His hand cupped her breasts and she turned in his arms, wrapping her legs around his waist before they broke the surface, panting for breath.

He watched the salt water bead and linger on the tips of her eyelashes. 'You know I want to kiss you.'

'I know.' She gave him a wicked grin and wriggled against him.

Despite the coolness of the water he instantly hardened.

'*Papá*, come.' Ignacio waved a shell he'd found.

He groaned quietly.

'That was your intention, right?' Lucy laughed.

'*Papá!* What shell. Is it?'

He shook his head, spraying her with water. 'You realise that you are destroying my credibility as a father.'

She flicked water back at him. 'Seeing you need a moment, I'll go and name the shell.'

'Okay.' But just before she moved away, he tenderly kissed her and she jerked against him, her eyes dilating into large inky discs. This time he laughed. 'Finding it hard to stand up?'

'Lucy. *Papá.* I'm hungry.'

Lucy gave him a thoughtful look. 'So this is what being a parent is like?'

He thought of how much fun he was having and how normal it all felt to be sharing what in essence was a family picnic. 'This is the easy part.'

She squeezed his hand and then they ran the short distance back to the shore together.

Lucy pulled on her running clothes, knowing she was cutting things very fine. 'Seeing Iggie's at Haven, will I bring him to the polo and meet you there?'

'Pardon?' Marco appeared in the doorway of the en suite, a white towel slung low on his hips and his torso with its dips and crevices on full display.

She dropped the shoe she was holding.

He winked at her and with a knowing look, he leaned his arm up against the wall, the movement flowing through toned muscles. He was the complete package—handsome, thoughtful, loving and caring—and she adored spending time with him and Iggie. Her heart hitched in her chest. She didn't want to think about how it was going to feel when she left Bulla Creek, left Marco and Iggie, but she knew she had to leave soon.

You could stay and join the practice.

The thought floated around her like a bubble of warmth and security and then it popped and reality dumped all over her. She didn't belong in Bulla Creek any more.

She didn't know where she belonged, which was why she'd put in an application to the UK. Surely it would be easier to be a stranger in a strange land rather than feeling like a stranger in a place where everybody knew her and considered she belonged. But even the idea of the UK didn't seem quite right and the thought gave her headache.

She picked up the shoe. 'You're so not playing fair. You know I don't have time to stay and take advantage of you.'

He pushed off the door and gathered her in his arms. 'You do realise that arriving at Haven all hot and sweaty having run from here pretending you were out for a morning jog is not fooling him. William knows.'

'No, he doesn't.' Her vehement words echoed around the room.

'He does.' Marco kissed her lightly on the lips. 'He has given me "the look".'

'What do you mean by that?'

'The look fathers give to the men their daughters date. The look that says, *Tread carefully and if you hurt her I will kill you.*'

She stooped down and tugged hard on her shoelaces, trying to get rid of the uncomfortable feeling that eddied inside her that William might know about her and Marco. She shrugged it away because William no longer had a say in her life, even if deep down she knew she wanted him to.

He'd forfeited the right. 'You don't have to worry because I'm not his daughter or his concern.'

His hand stroked the top of her head. 'Lucy, for your own peace of mind you need to forgive him.'

His quietly spoken words packed the punch of an exploding grenade and she shot to her feet. 'Oh, you mean just like you need to forgive Bianca?'

'This is not at all the same thing.' He pulled on his jodhpurs with a stiff jerk. 'Bianca does not love me or Ignacio. She does not belong in our lives but William loves you and belongs in yours. You grew up feeling loved, yes?'

Guilt, confusion and shame tangoed inside her as they often did. Yes, she'd had a loving and happy childhood and she knew she should be grateful but it was so hard to be when it turned out everything about her life had been predicated on huge, unspoken lies. 'I did but—'

'Trust the feeling.'

'I can't.'

Two lines appeared on the bridge of his nose. 'You have to. It is your lifeline through all of this.'

Was it? No. If the last six months had taught

her anything, it was that thinking about being adopted just made her miserable. People told her, 'You should be grateful you got great parents.' Did children raised by birth parents feel grateful? No one understood the emotional roller-coaster.

She took in a deep breath and shifted her focus to today and everything that hung on it being a success. Picking up his black and gold polo shirt, she threw it at him. 'Make sure you look as sexy as hell on that horse and strut your polo-playing skills. We need every reporter at the ground to notice you and Bulla Creek will do the rest.'

The tone of her voice and the jut of her chin told Marco he'd pushed her too far about William and he knew he'd chosen the wrong time to do it. Their picnic on the beach seemed a lifetime ago and the last five days in the run-up to the polo tournament had been huge, leaving them both strung out. Between his work as a doctor, his role as a father, the planning of the 'change the visa campaign' and being creative in finding convenient times when Ignacio was out of the house so he could make love to Lucy, he felt like he was four different people.

'Lucy.'

She jammed her cap on her head. 'What?'

He wasn't going to apologise but he didn't want her to leave angry either. Wrapping his arms around her rigid body, he pressed his lips to her ear and whispered, 'I promise to look as sexy as hell, but while I am doing it, I will be thinking of you.'

'Damn straight you will.' She lightly thumped his chest with her fist, and a smile creased her face. 'Iggie and I will be on the sidelines cheering you on.'

The thought of the two of them together made him smile.

'I don't think I can watch,' Lucy muttered as the fifth chukka came to an end with the score tied.

The weather couldn't have been more perfect if they'd been able to control it and the polo carnival was in full swing under a vivid blue sky. Black director's chairs with the sponsor's name stencilled in gold lined the edge of the field and behind them a large white marquee with its distinctive four 'steeples' served a never-ending supply of food, champagne and beer. The crowd was a mix of locals and people from Perth, and women in their fashionable best promenaded along the course, happy to have their photos taken for the social pages of the Perth papers. For the first time since arriving in Bulla Creek, Lucy was outclassed in footwear.

'*Papá* will get...' Ignacio took in a breath '...another goal.'

'I hope so.' Lucy tousled his hair as bitter longing rolled through her. She remembered having that sort of hero-worship for William and she hadn't lost it as a teenager like many children did. She'd lost it now though and she was struggling with the gaping hole its absence left in her life. Marco said, 'forgive' but it wasn't that straightforward. His life hadn't been stripped of history and connectedness. He still had family even though he'd chosen to live in Australia. He knew who he was.

She didn't.

William had been the reason she'd become a doctor because that's what the Pattersons had done down the generations. Only now she kept wondering what other career paths she might have taken if the expectation of medicine hadn't been held up to her for as long as she could remember. If she'd grown up with her real parents. The idea that her life could have been so very different, making her a different person completely, both taunted and perplexed her.

'Where is. William?' Ignacio turned in his chair, looking around at the crowd.

'He's meeting a friend.' Actually, he was having a beer with the local Member of Parliament, who he'd always had a good relationship with, and was trying to get some action happening to help Marco.

The thud of hooves against turf made Lucy look up and the pack of ponies thundered past, throwing up divots of grass as the sixth and final chukka commenced. As a child she'd belonged to the pony club but she'd never gained the skill of these horsemen who could control their mounts at the same time as leaning out sideways from the saddle and hitting a ball with a mallet. A polo pony needed heart, speed, stamina and the ability to turn on a penny. A good pony was eighty percent of the game.

The other twenty percent came from the player and Marco had that in spades. As expected, his dark, Latino presence on a thoroughbred horse made heads turn and cameras had been flashing all afternoon. They saw the way his muscular thighs gripped the saddle, how his tight behind rose and fell in perfect sync with the horse's movement and the power with which he hit the ball. She saw all that too, but she also saw a grace, determination and humility which flowed from the inside out and made her heart quiver in a way it never had before.

You love him.

No, I do not!

She gave herself a determined shake. No way was she falling in love. She couldn't. It wasn't her time. Not now with her own life in a total mess. Even though she hated the way Daniel had broken up with her, she now realised he had a point when he'd said she'd was emotionally cut off. She wasn't able to give enough so involving someone else wasn't a good idea. Especially a man with a child. With so many unanswered questions about her own mother, she could hardly be one herself. No, she was just in lust with Marco and it was all a temporary escape—from William, from the shambles of her life in Perth and the fog of her future. From everything.

As the final moments of the match counted down, sweat foamed on the coats of the hard-working horses and their tiring riders made some rookie mistakes. Supporters on both sides were biting their nails as the match stayed tied.

'If no one scores, they have to play another chukka,' she told Iggie. She'd expected him to lose interest in the match a long time ago, but he loved watching the horses and his father.

He stood up, leaving his crutches hanging on the chair. 'Go, *Papá*.' He waved his arms as Marco rode past and then he promptly listed sideways.

Lucy slipped her hand into his to steady him and his small fingers immediately closed around her palm. He grinned at her, his excitement palpable.

A rush of happiness so simple and pure poured through her and she grinned back. Raising their arms together, she yelled, 'Come on, Marco. Come on, Bulla Creek, you can do it.'

Marco wheeled his horse around and charged back down the field, his shirt billowing behind him as he chased down the white ball. He swung his arm out in a wide arc and his mallet hit it with a loud clack, sending it careening straight at goal. The number four player from the Perth team lunged from his saddle and blocked the ball.

Groans of despair mixed in with cheers of delight as the crowd revelled in the closeness of the game. Lucy didn't think her body could cope with much more adrenaline.

David Henderson was playing number three position and working hard to turn the play. Leaning from the near side of his pony, he shot the ball back toward his fellow Bulla Creek players. Marco saw the shot and urged his pony on, reaching the ball unopposed but at a sharp angle to goal. Reaching down and gripping the flexible bamboo shaft, he placed the mallet head behind the ball.

It was a tough shot and Lucy held her breath as the goal defence manoeuvred his horse into position.

Whack! Marco connected with the ball, sending it into a tight curve that shot straight through the goal posts.

'Yes!' Lucy screamed and punched the air and Iggie copied her, his face bright with delight.

Dizzy with excitement, she picked him up,

kissed him on the cheek and hugged him. 'We won, we won, we won.'

Iggie rested his head on her shoulder for a moment, his small, warm body relaxing against hers, and her heart cramped. Allison would have held her sons like this but never her.

She swallowed against the lump in her throat. If she ever had a child, she'd never let him go.

'Too tight.' Iggie wriggled in her arms.

With a start, she realised she was gripping the poor child so hard he could barely breathe. She put him down and patted his shoulder. 'Sorry, mate.'

The Bulla Creek crowd roared around them as the umpire blew his whistle, signalling the end of the match. The players rode off toward the saddling area and Lucy rose on her toes, craning her neck to see, but Marco had vanished into an appreciative crowd. She wanted to rush over to him and throw her arms around his neck in a congratulatory hug, but she didn't want to get in the way of the plan. Besides, Iggie couldn't 'rush' anywhere.

'Lucy?'

She squatted down so she was at Iggie's eye level. 'Yes, mate?'

'Can I.' He seemed to be concentrating harder than ever to get the words out. 'Ride a horse?'

'Ah...sure. I can't see why not.'

'Awesome.' His small body quivered with excitement. 'Can I do. It now?'

'Um.' She almost said 'no', because a polo pony was not the steed Iggie needed and then she saw David's wife, Tilly Henderson, and remembered that earlier in the day she'd seen her leading her three-year-old around on an old pony. 'Tilly.' She waved. 'Have you got a minute?'

Ten minutes later with a helmet on his head, Iggie was sitting on Betsy, with a grin on his face as wide as the world. Tilly led the pony and Lucy had her hand on Iggie's waist, supporting him like she'd seen Marco do when Iggie rode on his shoulders.

His legs which were so often tight because of spasming muscles relaxed and she didn't know if that was from the warmth of the horse or the movement or both. With each step the horse took, his hips tilted and Iggie sat up straighter. 'I want to try on my own.'

Lucy bit her lip, torn between wanting him to try and worried he might fall. 'Okay, but I'm going to have my hands just here, ready.'

'I won't need them.' His hands gripped the reins with a determination that seemed to hold him even straighter.

'I'm sure you won't but that's the deal.' She stayed close and he was remarkably steady as the movement of the horse flowed through him. His laughter and joy was infectious.

'I want to go faster.'

'One thing at a time, Iggie.'

Tilly turned around. 'Bets at a trot is still pretty slow, Lucy. You could jog next to him with your hand on him and then if he's steady move it to the back of the saddle.'

'Please, Lucy. I want to. Try.'

'I start all my riders on Bets,' Tilly said, 'and I haven't lost a customer yet. He's looking really comfortable and considering his unsteady legs, his rhythm is good. I have a friend down in Perth who provides the horses for therapy with kids—' she dropped her voice and mouthed '—worse than Iggie.'

A light bulb exploded in Lucy's head. 'Of

course. Hippotherapy.' Going by the expression on Iggie's face, it would be worth investigating for him. Gripping the back of the saddle, she said, 'Hold on tight, Iggie.'

Marco was hot and sweaty, smelt like horse and his mouth ached from smiling. He'd been thumped on the back by most of the men of Bulla Creek, kissed on the cheek by women he'd never met, but most importantly, he'd been able to tell his story to William's parliamentary friend. Now he was speaking with a television reporter. He knew this was important, but even so, he was drawing on all his patience to be charming and obliging and answering her questions fully about Ignacio and his own life when he was used to keeping things like that private. All he really wanted to do was find Lucy and kiss her hard and ask Ignacio what he thought of his *papá*'s winning goal.

'So your son?' The reporter asked with a smile. 'How old is he again?'

'Five. He is in first year of primary school.'

Her eyes lit up. 'Oh, cute age. Is he here today?'

Marco nodded. '*Sí*, he was watching the game

with my—' *Your what? Lover? Girlfriend?* 'A colleague and friend.'

The reporter flipped her notebook closed. 'Thanks, Marco, I think I've got all the information I need.'

A river of relief flowed through him that the interview was finally over. *'Gracias,* Patty.'

'All we need now is some footage of you and Ignacio together.'

His chest tightened. 'Is that necessary?'

'A picture tells a thousand words,' Patty quipped.

'I am happy to be filmed. You could—' Familiar laughter made him look beyond the reporter and his blood swooped to his feet. *'Querido Dios.'*

The reporter swung around to see what he was looking at. 'Is that your little boy on the horse?'

'Sí.' He strode directly to Ignacio with fear for his son and anger at Lucy burning in his veins.

He was only vaguely aware of Patty behind him saying, 'Come on,' and the ratting sound of equipment.

Ignacio's small hands gripped the reins as the

horse moved briskly toward them. '*Papá*, I'm just. Like you!'

'Be careful,' Marco yelled. 'Grip with your legs.' The moment the words left his mouth he knew how useless they were. His son didn't have the strength to do that. 'Stay still.'

Lucy's face was pink from her jog and she gave him a huge smile. 'Doesn't he look fantastic?'

He dropped his head close to hers and it took every ounce of control to keep his voice low. 'Did you lose your brain? He could have fallen and broken his neck.'

Incredulity shone stark on Lucy's face and her grey eyes flashed with the hurt of being misconstrued. 'You think I'd allow that? I would never put him in danger.'

He didn't want to listen to the voice inside him which agreed because he had evidence to the contrary in front of him.

She turned and spoke directly to Patty who'd arrived with a cameraman. 'Have you asked Dr Rodriguez about the benefits of hippotherapy for children with cerebral palsy? The movement of the horse flows though the child and it mimics the feel of walking. This adds to their physio-therapy with improved balance and gait.'

Her words ramped up his ire. He couldn't believe she had no clue she'd done something so inherently wrong. 'It is important that the parents give the permission for hippotherapy.'

Lucy's jaw shot up. 'Some parents are too scared to allow their children to take the therapy and by doing so hold their child back.'

His jaw locked with anger. 'Parents have rights.'

Lucy's faced blanched. 'So do children.'

Patty frowned, glancing between them, clearly confused. 'I'm sure this is all very interesting but right now this is the perfect picture we've been looking for. Pete needs to start filming if it's going to make the six o'clock news.'

The situation roared around him, growing into its own identity, totally disregarding his opinions and piling on top of the unease that he was losing control of his son and his life to other people.

This was *his* fight to stay in Australia and as much as he appreciated the support of the town and the power of the media, Ignacio shouldn't be part of it. 'Patty, I don't want—'

'Will I be. On TV?' Ignacio's eyes were wide

with wonder as he watched the fluffy boom microphone being positioned.

Lucy laid her hand on his arm. 'It's a *good* idea, Marco.'

He couldn't believe she'd just said that.

'Dad, if you stand next to the kid.' Pete started setting up the scene.

'I don't want Ignacio to be filmed.' The terse words exploded out of him making everyone stare at him in shocked surprise.

'I want to be. On television.' Ignacio's sweet voice sounded loud in the sudden silence. 'With you, *Papá.*'

Marco opened his mouth to say 'I'm not going to be on television' but Pete got in first.

'You don't want to disappoint the little guy especially as we've already got footage of you playing polo.' The cameraman grinned, knowing he'd just trumped the argument.

Bile rose in Marco's throat as the situation closed in on him. He could oblige or risk Ignacio having a tantrum, which they'd probably film anyway and that wouldn't paint him in a good light as a parent or a future citizen. In less than two minutes it would undo all the work of the previous week. He hated it that he'd been put in this position and he was furious with Lucy for siding with the press. Fathers were supposed to shield and protect their children, not sell them out by putting them on public display. *Dios*, he was pictorialising Ignacio's disability which was something he'd never wanted to do.

The cameraman said, 'Put your hand on the back of the saddle just like—'

'Lucy,' Ignacio offered up happily. 'Lucy found me. The horse. She's fun.'

A flash of green joined the rising bile. Ignacio needed an adult who knew what was best for him, not someone who acted first and thought second.

'Lucy, right.' Pete nodded. 'You don't mind stepping aside for a moment, do you?'

'Not at all.'

'An excellent idea.' Marco stepped in close to the pony.

'Just like hippotherapy.' Lucy moved sideways but her expression said she regretted nothing.

Marco swallowed a curse. She always had to have the last word but this time she'd gone too far.

She had no right to be making decisions about Ignacio. He gripped his son's waist.

'Ouch. *Papá*.' Ignacio wriggled away from his touch. 'Put your hand. On the saddle. Like Lucy.'

The green flare intensified. 'Lucy should have held onto you.'

His terse tone only made Ignacio more resolute. 'No. I can do it. On my own.'

'Smile, mate,' the cameraman said.

Knowing what was at stake, Marco got his lips to curve while he inwardly cursed the government and Lucy in that order.

CHAPTER TEN

LUCY had been called into the hospital to treat a horse handler who'd been kicked as he'd tried to load one of the polo ponies into a float. She'd been worried about the risk of cardiac tamponade, but thankfully it was only bruising of the chest wall. Even so, neither horse nor handler would be making the trip back to Perth tonight.

For the last two hours, she'd been trying to leave the hospital, but each time she picked up her bag someone else arrived who needed treatment, including two children sick with asthma. Now she'd finally got away and had driven straight to Marco's. She hadn't seen him since the television camera had stopped rolling and he'd taken Ignacio home without a backward glance.

That had been hours ago and they'd both had time to calm down. She'd been furious and hurt that he could think for a moment she'd put Ignacio in danger, but she now realised that his reaction had probably stemmed from the stress of the day and all the uncertainty around his future in Australia. She regretted the bitchy way she'd tried to involve the reporter in the argument and she planned to apologise. In fact, she was looking forward to spending an hour alone with Marco. It meant it would be past midnight by the time she got back to Haven, which was a good thing as William would be in bed.

Marco was outside, lying on the table with his hands behind his head, and she smiled, thinking how she could watch him for hours. A crazy feeling that almost resembled sadness came out of nowhere, curling through her, shocking her with its intensity. He looked so alone.

He needs someone to share the load.

An answering thought fluttered through her which she immediately scotched. They only shared sex. That was what they both wanted.

She bent down, brushing his lips with hers. 'So, are we going to add make-up sex to our repertoire?'

Instead of kissing her back, he sat up stiffly. 'You had no right to put Ignacio on a horse. I did not want him photographed and you knew that but you didn't care and you disregarded my opinion.'

She jerked back, totally blindsided by the intensity of his anger—an anger she'd assumed would have faded now he'd had time to think things through rationally. 'Hang on just a minute, those two things are not remotely connected.'

Despite trying to find calm, she couldn't keep the incredulity out of her voice. 'You think I put Ignacio on the horse for a PR stunt?'

His stony expression didn't flicker. 'Yes.'

Did he really have such a small amount of regard for her?

Why not?

The traitorous voice of doubt that had plagued her since she'd found out she was adopted boomed in her head. *Allison didn't want you and William didn't think you deserved your own life story.* The tremble of rejection started at her toes and like wildfire driven by a hot wind, it whipped through her, consuming all of her in a second. 'It was sheer coincidence that Iggie arrived on a horse.'

Rejection morphed into fury. 'But you know what? You should be thanking me because it was the ultimate PR coup and we couldn't have hoped for better. Iggie was as cute as a button sitting astride that old pony looking like every other five-year-old, and *not* a drain on the public health system. It got you on the news, giving you the coverage you need. It's all about exposure.'

His hand slapped the table. 'Using my son is not what I wanted and now I have more reporters wanting to intrude on his life.'

'Good. It will only help your cause. Let's hope the immigration minister saw the news too.' Her anger deflated as fast as it had come and she sighed. 'Marco, you're not using Iggie. If it helps, think about it this way. He loved being on TV and he's a natural in front of the camera so you haven't scarred him for life. He wanted to do it. I understand you want to shelter him from a media circus, but this isn't one so stop being so hard on yourself.'

She traced his cheek with her finger, aching for him and the fact he'd had to parent Ignacio on his own for so long and deal with all the extra things that a child with a disability brought into the mix. She wanted to lighten his load. 'Think of it as broadening his experiences. He loved watching you play polo and he wanted to share part of the experience. At least I think that's why he asked me if he could ride a horse. He was desperate to try it.'

He cupped her wrist and brought her hand down from his face. 'And if he asked to play on the road would you say "yes"?'

'Oh, come on, Marco.' She slapped her hands against her hips. 'That is a ridiculous thing to say. I was next to him the whole time just like a therapist would be if he rode each week. Can you honestly tell me that if he'd asked you if he could ride a horse you would have said no?'

His face remained intransigent. 'He's seen me play polo many times and he's never once asked me if he could ride a horse. If he did I would have told him he needed to be older.'

But Ignacio getting older wouldn't change anything. It was like pieces in a puzzle suddenly slotting together to show the full picture and it looked like fear. 'This is just like the soccer ball.'

Marco's shoulders stiffened. 'If you mean you should not be making decisions for Ignacio then, yes.'

'Actually, that's not what I meant at all.' She let his comment roll over her and sat down next to him, wanting to touch him, wanting to make him understand. 'Marco, like I told you earlier, I'd never put Iggie in danger, but he needs experiences. I don't think you wrapping him in cotton wool is healthy.'

He frowned. 'What do you mean by cotton wool?'

'Over-protecting.'

'You don't know what you are talking about.' The words came out tight and guarded. 'I provide him with therapy so he can improve, so how is that over-protecting him?'

She stroked his arm with her hand. 'I don't think you *mean* to do it.'

'I don't need to know what you think, Lucy.'

His accent usually caressed her name, but this time it came out as a warning growl. The hair on the back of her neck stood up.

Back off now before you get hurt.

But she couldn't because every part of her said, *Open his eyes and help him understand. Fight for Ignacio.*

It's not your fight.

Yes, it is. I love them both too much to let this ride. Her breath solidified in her lungs. Oh, God, she loved them. *No, no, please, no.* It was too soon, it was the wrong place and the wrong time, but her heart was deaf to it all.

Love propelled her onward. 'Marco, if Ignacio didn't have CP you'd be pushing him harder, but fear is making you play it safe. What if safety is the worst thing for him? What if you keep him so safe he never achieves his potential? What if you're so busy protecting him you don't give him the opportunity to strive and try harder?' She gulped in a quick breath and slid her hand into his. 'Hippotherapy is wonderful for helping with balance. It improves all movement and as Iggie adored being on the horse so much he'd get even more out of it.'

He withdrew his hand. 'I think I know what is best for *my* son.'

'I'm not sure that you do.' She rushed on, trying to get through to him. 'I'm only saying this because I love you both and if Iggie was my son, I'd be signing him up for a weekly session and watching him blossom.'

Oh, God, what did you just say?

Marco's eyes widened in shock. 'You do *not* love us.'

She wrung her hands, horrified that the words had slipped out. 'I do and believe me, it's as much of a shock to me as it is to you.'

'I don't want to be loved, Lucy. Not that way and you're so confused about your life that I think you are confused about loving us. I know you're upset that your birth mother and her family don't want you in their lives, but you have a family with William who loves you.' He ran his hand through his hair. 'Ignacio and I can't be your family.'

We can't be your family.

His words sliced deep into her naive and unsuspecting heart, the one she should have protected, and she bit her lip against the wave of pain. The metallic taste of blood hit her tongue.

She should have known better. She should have been more alert, more on guard. Now she'd just allowed more pain to pile up on the cairn that was currently her life. She scrambled to her feet. 'You've made yourself very clear, Marco.'

Tension held him captive but anguish flared in his eyes. 'I needed to.'

She tilted her chin, trying to hold back bitter

tears. 'I think we're way past the point of make-up sex, don't you? This is the end of our road.'

'*Sí*, it is.'

Her heart wept and she walked to the gate. When she reached it, she turned back slowly, determined to leave with some dignity intact. 'Most of it's been fun. This last bit not so much.'

His face twisted. 'Lucy, be kind to yourself. Take some time to answer all the questions that are plaguing you so you can live your life without regrets.'

She didn't want to hear that. 'Goodbye, Marco.' She closed the gate behind her.

Lucy sat at the kitchen table with a throw rug over her shoulders, her knees pulled up to her chin and her hands wrapped around a coffee mug. She was watching the dawn break and the golden fingers of sunlight spreading across the sky. She hadn't gone to bed, there'd have been no point. Awake or asleep her mind was reliving every heart-breaking moment of her conversation with Marco from the instant she'd realised she loved him to the second he'd shut her out of his life.

Shut out like her birth mother had shut her out. 'Problem, possum?'

Her heart, already wrung out to the point of dryness, managed to bleed a little more. She hadn't heard William call her by her pet name since the morning of Ruth's funeral and with a jolt of shock she realised she'd missed it.

She gulped coffee, not having expected to feel that way. Why did everything to do with William have to be bitter-sweet? It was exhausting and nothing would induce her to talk to him about Marco. She didn't confide in him any more.

'It's nothing. Why are you up so early?'

'Couldn't sleep.' He limped over to her and sat down, his face drawn like it had been when she'd first arrived. It was in stark contrast to his healthier glow of the last two weeks and she felt a twinge of concern.

'I've known you all your life, Lucy, and it doesn't look like nothing.' He poured himself a coffee from the pot and took a sip. 'You sitting there all curled up reminds me of the time you and Phoebe Henderson took the car and crashed it into McCurdy's ditch.'

She remembered that. Phoebe's then boyfriend

had been throwing a party on a nearby property but Phoebe hadn't been allowed to attend. Phoebe had turned up at Haven in tears and had convinced Lucy she should drive her, levering the fact that a boy Lucy had liked at the time would be there and if she didn't go to the party he would end up with Chloe Hogarth. The sixteen-year-old logic had seemed flawless right up until the car had hit gravel and spun out of control.

God, she'd been so scared—scared she'd hurt herself and Phoebe, and then scared to tell William because she didn't want to see his disappointment of her shining bright in his eyes. The memory stirred up a question that had played on her mind ever since she'd discovered her adoption papers. Maybe it was the quiet of the dawn or her ragged emotions, but she thought things couldn't get any worse. 'Were there times like that when you regretted adopting me?'

William gasped, his face twisting with sorrow. 'Never. Not one single moment. Your mother and I loved you from the moment we laid eyes on you and you've always been, and always will be, my pride and joy. Why would you doubt that?'

'Because of the lie.' Her voice broke. 'Can't you

see it casts doubt on everything? I trusted you implicitly. You were always the person I took my problems to and yet you did this to me.' A rogue tear escaped, rolling down her cheek. 'Why? I can't get around it. I can't forgive you for that.'

William shuddered. 'You're right, it's un-forgiveable. What we did was wrong and I've known it was wrong from the moment I reluc-tantly agreed not to tell you.'

Startled, she thought she must have misheard. 'You agreed not to tell me? Agreed with who?'

Despite the cool of the early morning, sweat beaded on William's brow. 'Your mother.'

She almost said, 'Which one?', but the question was futile because to William she'd only ever had one mother and that was Ruth. Truth be told, Ruth *was* the only mother she would ever have. Bitter pain twisted through her and she heard herself say, 'My birth mother sent a letter and it turns out you were right all along. She asked me not to contact her again.'

'Oh, Lucy.' His hand reached out and hovered above hers as if he was wondering how his touch would be received and then he briefly squeezed it. His grief flowed into her, melding with her own. 'I'm so sorry. I know how much you wanted a connection with her and with Ruth gone it was even more—'

His shoulders slumped but then he seemed to gather himself. 'Ruth and I had always dreamed of a large family but as you know, she had several miscarriages due to her diabetes. When we had the opportunity to adopt you, we were in seventh heaven. From the moment she held you in her arms and you wrapped your tiny hand around her finger she was your mother.'

Marco's voice drifted across her mind. *When you hold your baby in your arms there is such a surge of love and protection that it changes you.* 'But that doesn't explain why she didn't want to tell me I was adopted.'

'She was scared.' The simple words hung in the air. 'Perhaps because she'd lost so many babies she couldn't quite believe you were hers to keep and her biggest fear was losing you. She was a tigress in her protection of you. She begged me to support her in keeping your adoption a secret.'

William loves you and you need to forgive him. Lucy sat back in her chair, fighting to reconcile love with secrecy and trust with misguided loyalty. 'Did you ever question it?'

His eyes filled with distress. 'I loved you both too much to risk making either of you unhappy and I justified it as protection, but it's a decision that's eaten at me for years. The way you found out haunts me every day.'

'You sound just like Marco.' The words slipped out on a sea of heartache. 'What is it about parents and misguided protection?'

Astonishment flooded William's face quickly followed by understanding. 'So this is why you're huddled up here? You and Marco had a lovers' tiff?'

Tiff so seriously understated what had gone down between them that her stomach cramped. 'We're not lovers.'

'I have eyes, Lucy.'

She sighed, knowing she'd rarely ever got anything past him. 'Put it this way then. We're no longer lovers or even friends. He told me in no uncertain terms I'm not part of his life and he's furious with me for suggesting he's over-protecting Iggie. Having been over-protected, I think I know what I'm talking about.'

His normally mild hazel eyes flashed in his pale face as he momentarily rubbed his chest. 'Did I ever hold you back from what you wanted to do?'

Her instant response of 'You lied to me' rose to her lips, but something in his gaze made her set that aside and she thought about all the opportunities she'd been given. 'No.' She bit her lip as everything rushed back. 'Did you ever plan to tell me I was adopted after Ruth died?'

'Yes.' He nodded slowly. 'I was going to tell you the day after the funeral. I know this isn't any consolation, but please know that your mother only ever wanted you to feel loved. She *never* wanted you to feel the way I can only imagine you've been feeling since she died.'

Long held-back tears spilled over. 'I love you both but I hate how all of this has made me feel. I have this great, big empty hole inside me like I'm not good enough and that my life isn't mine.'

'We failed you.' Utter desolation lined his face and he suddenly gasped. His already pale face went from white to ashen grey as one hand gripped his chest and the other reached out to her.

Fright tore through her. Had she just reached a

point where they might be able to move forward only to have him die? 'Dad? Do you have pain down your arm?'

He could barely speak. 'Can't. Breathe. SVT.'

'What?' Incredulously, she pressed her fingers against his neck. Stress could cause it but she didn't trust self-diagnosis especially with such a sudden and unexpected onset. How would he even know he had super ventricular tachycardia?

His pulse pounded so hard it was almost too fast to count but after ten seconds she rapidly multiplied. 'Two hundred beats per minute. I'm going to try vagus nerve massage.'

William barely nodded as her fingers started massaging his neck near his trachea. The plan was to stimulate the release of chemicals and break the abnormal electrical circuit in the heart which had triggered the SVT. A minute later his heart was still galloping out of control.

'Don't move.' She shot to her feet and tore down the hall to his study where he kept his medical bag.

When she got back William was leaning back in his chair gulping in short, shallow breaths.

Oh, God, no. Lucy's fear for William—fear for

herself—escalated. If she didn't slow his heart down fast, his blood pressure would plummet and he'd be at a risk of cardiac failure and anoxia of the brain. 'I'm going to give you adenosine.'

Hardly able to speak, William closed his eyes as if saying yes. The drug had to be given intravenously and she wrapped a tourniquet around his arm, pulling it tight and then started tapping for the feel of a vein. Her fingers begged for the worm-like rise as her eyes scanned for the trademark blue wiggle.

Nothing. *Stay calm.* 'I'll try your other arm.'

Whipping the tourniquet off, she tried his left arm but she could see tiny scars on his inner elbow as if others before her had tried and failed to find a decent vein when he wasn't peripherally shut down. She checked his pulse again. Two hundred and twenty.

She had to act fast. 'Stay with me, Dad. I've got one more idea.'

She raced into the kitchen and with the crash of baking pans and wire cake coolers tumbling out onto floor, she hauled out the huge stainless steel basin Ruth had always used when she made the Christmas cake. Filling it with ice and cold water, she carried it quickly back to the table, sloshing water everywhere.

William's frantic gaze met hers. She bit her lip, put her hand on the back of his head and said, 'Okay, you know the drill. Hold your breath.' She pushed his head down to the freezing water.

He jerked as the cold hit him and she kept her hand firmly on his head, keeping him in place and she counted to four. *Please let this work.*

She pulled at his hair and William sat up gasping and coughing, and Lucy wished she had a towel to give him but the most important thing was to take his pulse. Her fingers pressed against neck and his pulse thundered under her fingers still fast but stronger. Her legs trembled as relief flowed through her. 'One hundred and hopefully dropping. Thank goodness for the diving reflex. Are you feeling a bit better?'

His hand found hers. 'I can get my breath and my heart no longer feels like it's going to bounce out of my chest. Thank you, sweetheart.'

She gave him a weak smile and checked his pulse again. 'Eighty. I think we've won for now. I'll get you some dry clothes to warm you up and then I'm inserting a butterfly so we have an open vein. Then you're going to the hospital and as soon as I can arrange it, you're going to Perth attached to a cardiac monitor.'

'You're my daughter. Tell Marco and he can arrange it.'

Her heart cramped. Her plan had been to leave for Perth this morning and never see or talk to Marco again. 'Surely I can refer you to a cardiologist in Perth.'

William looked sheepish. 'I already have one.'

Betrayal mixed in with indignation. 'And Marco knows and neither of you told me?'

William sighed. 'Marco doesn't know and I didn't tell you because I didn't want you to come to Bulla Creek out of duty. I wanted you to come back because you *wanted* to see me. But Marco contacted you and duty brought you back.'

'And you kept extending my stay.' She thought about how tired he'd often looked, how he'd been slow to return to work and how he'd self-diagnosed, only it hadn't been self-diagnosis after all. 'Those anti-hypertensive tablets are yours, aren't they?'

He grimaced. 'Yes.'

'If you've known you have SVT for a while, I don't understand why the cardiologist hasn't inserted a pacemaker already?'

'I haven't seen the cardiologist.'

She slapped her forehead with the palm of her hand thinking that doctors—male doctors—made the worst patients. 'Why on earth not?'

'Up until today, the episodes have only lasted a couple of minutes and I put the dizziness, anxiety and occasional runs of palpitations down to stress.' He started to shiver. 'Given the year we've had, that wasn't such an outrageous assumption.'

'Oh, Dad, I'm sorry. I've been so caught up with how I've been feeling that I pinned all my feelings of anger onto you. That wasn't fair and I totally missed that this whole mess has been as tough on you as it has been on me.'

'I love you, Lucy. You're my sun, moon and stars and I'm just glad you're here.'

She hugged him hard, feeling his arms tight around her just as they'd always been when she'd been a child and one hand patting her back. A shiver rocked through her and she realised that water had seeped through her T-shirt and onto her skin. 'We need to get you dry.'

She organised towels and clothes and while William changed, she rang the ambulance and Deb at the hospital. The nurse offered to contact Marco and Lucy accepted, not having the energy to face him.

As she slid the tourniquet onto William's arm, he put his other hand on her hair, just like he had when she'd been a little girl. 'Always know that you're a wonderful doctor, Lucy, and a true Patterson.'

'Only we both know that's not strictly true.' She wiped his arm with an alcohol swab. 'If at eighteen I'd said I wanted to be an artist, what would you have said?'

Surprise lit across William's face. 'You have many talents, darling, but drawing isn't one of them. Besides, you always said you wanted to be a doctor.'

She expertly slid the butterfly needle into his arm. 'I know, but that's because I thought medicine ran in my veins. Now I'm not so sure and I keep wondering what I might have done, who I might have been, if you were not my father.'

A tremor ran through him. 'Then go and find out.'

Stunned, she looked up from taping the needle. 'Really?'

A look of utter defeat crossed his face. 'The truth is that I've always hoped and dreamed you'd join the Bulla Creek practice, and when I saw you falling in love with Marco, I hoped against hope you'd stay.'

'He doesn't love me.'

'Well, he's a fool, but we're often fools when it comes to love.'

'I'm so confused, Dad.'

He sighed and squeezed her hand. 'Your mother's and my secret has caused you so much anguish and as much as I want you to stay, I don't want you here out of duty. If this feeling of "Who am I?" is tormenting you so much then go and find out. I only want you to be happy.'

Take some time to answer all the questions that are plaguing you so you can live your life without regrets.

The image of Marco and Iggie loomed in her mind and on a surge of pain, she shut them out. They didn't figure in her future and even if they did, both Marco and William were right. Before she could move forward, she had to find out who she really was.

CHAPTER ELEVEN

THE clock chimed three and Marco's stomach grumbled reminding him he hadn't had lunch. It had been a hellish few days. William was in Perth recovering from having a pacemaker inserted and Lucy had gone south with him. He'd spoken to William on the phone in Perth. The elder doctor had told him he'd be home in two days, back at work in two weeks.

William had also added that he was sorry but Marco would have to cope without a locum during that time. This meant Lucy wasn't returning to Bulla Creek. He grabbed a handful of sugar-coated chocolates he kept in a jar on his desk to encourage uncooperative children into thinking that he wasn't a bad guy.

An image of Lucy's grey eyes filled with hurt and pain seared him. He shovelled more candy into his mouth. He'd never wanted to cause her any anguish or suffering, but how could he not when she'd broken their self-imposed rules by thinking she'd fallen in love with him? He didn't want to be loved—not in a way that meant marriage and a partnership. He and Ignacio were fine on their own and that was why he'd spent years keeping women at bay.

Regret that he'd inflicted pain surged again, just as it had every day since Lucy had walked out and his gate had thudded shut behind her. He should have known better than to get involved with her when she was so emotionally vulnerable, but she'd got under his skin like no one else ever had. She made him laugh, she made him hungry for life, but at the same time she had no hesitation in getting involved in things that didn't concern her—like Ignacio—and telling him in no uncertain terms when she disagreed with him. Not even Bianca had done that.

Bianca didn't care though.

The thought rattled him just like all thoughts of Lucy and he squared his shoulders. It was time to stop thinking about her and get on with his life. He had a visa battle to win and he couldn't afford more days of feeling spun out and emotionally shell-shocked. Whatever it was that had swirled between the two of them, creating an irresistible force which pulled them together with the strength of a magnet, it had come to an end. He was back to being alone again which was how he liked it and how he needed it to be. He and Ignacio against the world and his heart safely intact.

He stood up in preparation to call his next patient but as he reached the door his phone rang. He doubled back to answer it. 'Marco Rodriguez.'

'Hi, Marco, it's Pippa Martin, Ignacio's physiotherapist.'

He'd put Ignacio on the bus earlier with Heather and the other children as it was a Geraldton therapy day. 'Yes, Pippa. Is something wrong?'

She laughed. 'Why do parents always go there first? Nothing's wrong and Iggie's doing great. His walking in today's session was the best I've ever seen it and I was wondering if you'd tried something new since I saw him last week?'

Last week had been beyond busy, full of town meetings, preparing for the polo match, a normal clinic load and Ignacio's parent-teacher night. *And making love to Lucy.*

He disregarded the last thought. 'It was an unusual week and to tell you the truth I did not have time to do the extra—' A thought exploded in his head, sucking the words from his mouth.

'Marco?' Pippa sounded concerned. 'Is it an okay time to talk?'

Her voice was just a faint echo because his mind had been whipped back to the polo, seeing Ignacio sitting on the horse, feeling fear making his heart leap in his chest and hearing Lucy say, 'The movement of the horse mimics the feel of walking and improves balance and gait.' He swallowed and tried to relax his throat. 'Ignacio rode a horse on Saturday.'

'Awesome. Keep it up.' Pippa's enthusiasm poured down the phone. 'You know I've been trying to start hippotherapy but we need horses and funding. I saw you on the news playing polo so you've obviously got horse contacts and I'd love it if you'd join a committee to help get this project off the ground.'

His head spun. 'I may not be in Australia much longer.'

She laughed. 'Marco, you've been all over the media for five days talking up the need for rural GPs and how Ignacio is a valued member of the community. The Bulla Creek district has deluged

the immigration department with emails and pe-
titions, and this morning on the radio I heard the
health minister saying the ruling against you was
"a disgrace" and that Australia needs doctors of
your calibre.'

He'd heard it too and hope had risen but reality
had immediately levelled it. 'She is not the immigration minister and he is the one that makes
the final decision.'

'True, but she's one heck of a strong-minded
woman and I can just picture her stomping across
the pale green carpet at Parliament House and
storming into the minister's office to give him a
piece of her mind.'

Lucy's earnest face rose in his mind. *If Iggie
was my son, I'd be signing him up for a weekly
session and watching him blossom.*

'I'll let you go, Marco, but if you can get
Ignacio on a horse for half an hour each week,
that's really going to help him. The moment
your visa's approved, I'm co-opting you onto the
"Freedom Riders" committee.'

The phone went dead and he sat down abruptly,
his legs suddenly unsteady. *Dios.* Lucy had been
right all along. He'd been so furious at her for

what he saw as her undermining his rights as Ignacio's father and scared for his son that he hadn't wanted to hear her, but he'd been doing the exact thing she'd accused him of. He was letting fear get in the way of what was best for his son. He ploughed both hands through his hair. How long had he been doing that? From the beginning? *No.* That couldn't be.

I provide him with therapy so he can improve, so how is that over-protecting him?

His self-righteous words to Lucy boomed in his head with horrifying clarity and he knew he could no longer ignore them. For too long he'd used those words to justify the fact he always chose the safest path for Ignacio. He challenged him academically but he always shied away from extra physical activities beyond his therapy.

I'd never put him in any danger. I love him.

His chest tightened. Lucy had been the brave one. She'd taken the fight for Ignacio to the next level, recognising he was growing up and needing that sort of stimulation. No wonder Ignacio had been getting cross with him and railing against his cosseting. Lucy hadn't let fear get in the way and as a result she'd opened up Ignacio's world. He'd thrived under that sort of love.

You thrived too.

He dropped his head into his hands as the truth was laid out bare. He hadn't wanted to admit it to himself but he could no longer deny it. He'd hidden behind his anger since she'd left, but he knew it was because accepting that he missed her would rupture the bubble he'd locked his heart in since Bianca's betrayal. That had scared the hell out of him.

But thrived he had and he thought of how well they'd worked together, exchanging ideas, learning from each other and growing as doctors. He couldn't deny the caring way she'd rallied the town behind him to help him fight the visa decision, but with her sense of social justice, he knew she would have done that for anyone in his position. What he treasured most were the picnics, the shared meals, the conversations in his bed when she'd rested her head on his chest and her hair tickled his nose—the everyday things— that had given him moments of peace unlike he'd ever known.

That's love.

Every part of him stalled in shock. *Love is too risky.*

Lucy is everything that Bianca is not.

He knew that as well as he knew that the sky was blue and the earth was round. His breath rushed out and the years of being alone rolled away.

He loved Lucy.

You told her you didn't want her in your life.

He'd admit to stupidity, apologise and hold her tight. He wanted her in his life, wanted her to be part of Ignacio's life and he wanted it all to start now.

He just had to find her.

Lucy stared at the twelve boxes that were sealed up with brown packing tape and represented the end of an era of her living in Perth, and sharing a house with the woman who'd been her friend. 'Jess, the removal van will be here in an hour and...' she wound a key off her key ring '...this is yours.'

Jess twisted her hands. 'I hate what I did to our friendship, Luce.'

'Yeah, I know.' Lucy rubbed her dust-covered

forehead, feeling grimy and tired after a day of packing. 'Dan and I had hit the wall, but it still hurt. It hurt a lot.'

'Do you think you can ever forgive me?' Jess asked in a small voice.

'I think just recently I've learned that forgiveness isn't so much about wiping the slate clean and going back to the way things were, but about moving forward and forging a new way of doing things.'

Relief flooded Jess's face. 'So you're going to be okay about Dan and me?'

'Yes, I am. That said, I'm not quite ready to have dinner with the two of you, but you never know. Maybe after I get back from India.'

'Thanks.' Jess moved in and hugged her. 'I can't believe you've pulled all your registrar applications and you're just taking off. I just hope you find what you're looking for.'

Lucy didn't want to try and explain that it wasn't about finding any more but about learning, so she just hugged her back.

The doorbell rang and Lucy checked her watch. 'Wow, removalists who are actually early.'

Jess gave her a quick kiss goodbye, slung her

bag onto her shoulder and said, 'I'll leave you to it.'

Lucy started marking the boxes with a black felt pen and she heard the murmur of voices and Jess saying, 'Go straight down the hall.'

As the tread of footsteps got louder, she straightened up saying, 'You can start with—' The pen slipped from her fingers, rolling across the floor to stop at Marco's dusty boots.

'*Hola, Lucy.*'

He stood in front of her wearing dark blue slim-fit jeans that emphasised his long legs, and a pale blue casual shirt with the sleeves rolled up, exposing tanned skin and the veins and tendons of his powerful forearms. Her heart flipped in her chest before she could wrap it up safely in protective foil. 'You're a long way from Bulla Creek.'

Tension held his cheeks hostage but his eyes sought hers. 'I came to see you.'

She swallowed against the traitorous pull of her body which craved to feel the security of his length lining hers and she resisted the urge to step into his arms. She knew that until she was able to stand alone and feel whole she couldn't seek him out. It wouldn't be fair to him and

Ignacio. Besides, he didn't want her. The memory of his unyielding stance the last time she'd seen him, combined with his transparent words, were impossible to misinterpret.

Crossing her arms to steady herself, she tilted her chin. 'Why? Need some more help with the visa problem, do we?'

He flinched as if her words had inflicted a wound of their own. 'I came here to apologise. I was wrong.'

Stay strong. 'You were wrong about a lot of things. Which one in particular?'

'About Ignacio. You were right. I have been sheltering him too much from his life.'

She sat down abruptly on a box before her legs gave way and deposited her unceremoniously on the floor at his feet. She hadn't expected that confession and confusion got tangled up with all her other feelings. Crossing her legs, she bounced a gladiator-sandal-clad foot up and down to help her think.

His hungry gaze followed the movement and she quickly uncrossed her legs, pressing both feet firmly against the floor. Desire had no place between them. Not any more. 'Well, it's good that you've finally worked it out but you didn't need to come seven hundred kilometres to tell me.'

'*Sí*, I did.'

'And why is that?'

He moved toward her but she pushed out her hands like two red stop signs. It was hard enough to think with him in the room without him being so close that his vibrant scent of pure soap and citrus eddied around her, reminding her of everything she'd lost.

He paused unhappily a few feet away from her. 'Because you're the one person who pushed me and opened my eyes to what I was doing. I have been letting fear get in the way of Ignacio becoming the best person he can be.' His fingers ran though his hair as if he was pulling the words out one by one. 'His mother didn't love him and I didn't want him to feel he isn't enough for me as he is.'

Her heart twisted for Ignacio and herself. Both of them had birth mothers who couldn't love them, but at least Marco had worked out how damaging over-protection was while Ignacio was young enough to forget the pain it caused. She wished her adopted mother had. 'He's a lucky boy.'

His gaze searched her face. 'He is because of you.'

Waves of pain radiated through her and she rose to her feet not wanting to think about his beautiful little boy because it hurt too much. 'I'm glad I could help and now you've got that off your chest, you need to go. I have to finish writing on these boxes.' She bent down to pick up the felt pen and as she rose, his long, lean fingers closed gently around her wrist.

'I *love* you, Lucy.'

Her grey eyes filled with shock, quickly followed by something Marco couldn't exactly name. It sent a chill scudding through him.

Glancing down at his hand on her arm, she then looked back at him. 'What happened to "I don't want to be loved"?'

Honesty was all he had to offer. 'I was wrong about that too.'

She stared at him coolly as if his words hadn't penetrated at all. 'So what are you actually saying?'

On the flight down to Perth, he'd run a variety of scenarios through his head and all of them had pictured Lucy being initially upset with him, but falling into his arms the moment he told her he loved her. Right now she looked as far away from doing that as Bulla Creek was from Perth. A tremor of panic started to build.

Catching her hands with his, he said, 'Come back to Bulla Creek with me.'

She stared at him wordlessly, her face contorted with suffering and then she spun out of his reach and disappeared into another room.

His heart paused—suspended in mid-beat for a long, pain-filled moment—and then it thundered hard and fast, sending desperation scudding through him. He strode in the same direction and found her leaning against the kitchen sink, gulping down a glass of water.

'Lucy, I do not understand. Less than a week ago you told me you loved me.'

She slowly raised her head and the agony in her eyes pierced him. 'I do love you. And Ignacio. I love you both more than I can say.'

'Gracias a Dios.' Relief poured through him and he closed the gap between them, sweeping her into his arms.

She leaned in against him, resting her head under his shoulder the way she always did but then she dragged in a shuddering breath. 'I can't come back to Bulla Creek with you, Marco. Like you said, it's all happened too early and too fast.'

'So we will go slowly and take our time.' He gently gripped her upper arms and moved her slightly away from him so he could see her face. He needed her to see his, to read his regret and now his hope.

'I was a fool and I was wrong. Your love for me and Ignacio was like the force of a tornado, swooping in and knocking us off our feet, and at first I was terrified of letting myself love you back. But life with you is so much better than without you. You have woken my heart from hibernation.'

She stared at his shoulder. 'Bianca hurt you and Iggie very much and I don't want you rushing into a relationship worried that I'll leave like she did.'

'That isn't going to happen. You're nothing like Bianca. You wear your heart on your sleeve and are one of the most giving persons I've ever met.' He believed that with every fibre of his being and he pulled her back close, stroking her hair. 'I've been letting the past be my present, but sharing the last few weeks with you and Ignacio have been the happiest times in my life and my heart is yours. I want to share my life with you.'

She bit her lip and he held his breath, thinking, hoping, that by reminding her of what they'd experienced together she'd change her mind.

She stepped back from him and drank more water. Slowly, she put the glass down on the bench as if she was carefully formulating her reply. 'I've had almost a week to think and something you said to me, about me looking for a family—'

'I promise you that Ignacio and I are your family. You are his mother.' Words tumbled urgently from his mouth to both stop her from speaking and to force her to change her mind. 'William is your family and my parents, when they arrive, they too are your family. Bulla Creek is your family. Everyone who loves and cares for you is there.'

She shook her head. 'I've spent the last six months wondering who I am and as much as I love you I've realised that if I don't work through this, it will eventually destroy us. *I* will destroy us. It's why I'm going to India.'

India. His blood plummeted to his feet as he remembered the boxes in the other room. 'For how long?'

Tears shone in her eyes. 'For as long as it takes.'

No. 'We will come with you.'

Her face filled with a tortured understanding. 'Like you've always said, this is something I have to do on my own and even if it wasn't, with all this visa stuff, you can't leave Australia at the moment. Besides, Ignacio doesn't belong in the foothills of the Himalayas and I wouldn't do that to him. I love him too much.'

'Then stay. Don't do this to us. To me.' He heard the anguish in his voice coming straight from his heart. 'I need you.'

'Do you think—?' Her voice broke and she reached out, touching his arm. 'Do you think I'd be leaving you and Ignacio if I had a choice?'

Desperation drove him on. 'Of course you have a choice. You say, "Marco, I am not going to India, I am coming home to Bulla Creek with you where I belong".'

She tugged at her hair as tears fell. 'I was taking my love for you with me to India to learn how to deal with it. You weren't supposed to turn up here telling me you loved me and making everything harder. This wasn't part of the plan.'

He saw a chink in her resolution and hope surged. Wiping away her tears, he said, 'There is nothing to deal with. I love you. I'm sorry it took me so long to realise that, but I am here now. We have a life together. *This* is the moment you change your plans.'

Sobbing, she shook her head. 'I want to but I can't. You told me that if I didn't forgive William it would haunt me. You also said I should take some time to answer all the questions that are plaguing me so I can live my life without regrets. I can't do it here. I have to go away and India offers me the place to still my churning mind so I can start the search of who I am. I'm sorry but I *have* to do this.'

The memory of his well-meant words taunted him, and he couldn't believe he'd been the architect of her plan that was now taking her away from him. The resolve in her voice left him without a single doubt that she was going to India and dread made him beg. Hugging her tightly as if he thought she might vanish immediately, he said, 'I don't want you to go. Please stay.'

'It's not that simple, Marco.' She hiccoughed, wiping her face against his shirt. 'I keep asking myself am I the person I'm supposed to be? How can I be part of your life, part of Ignacio's if I don't know that?'

Tears built behind his eyes as he struggled to fight something that towered over him like a fire-breathing dragon protecting the treasure he desperately wanted and he had no sword strong enough to slay it. 'Stay here and try new things. If you don't want to work as a doctor any more so be it. Take a course, sell houses, I don't mind. Just know that whatever you do, you are the woman I love. It is enough.'

She cupped his cheek gently and her grey eyes swam with pleading. 'If I don't go, it will fester and damage us and I won't allow that. Please understand that I'm doing this not just for me but for us. For Ignacio. I never want to put the two of you through the pain of us failing because I was emotionally distant wondering who I am. I have to do this or we'll regret it for the rest of our lives.'

He gripped her hand as if the pressure would

change her mind. 'You going to India is abandoning us.'

'No, it's saving us. Short term pain for long term gain. *Please* understand.'

The irony that he'd been the one to push her to deal with her adoption lay at his feet and defeat licked at his heels. He finally knew that if he wanted her in his life forever, he had to let her go to India, but he hated the idea. 'I will phone you every day.'

She shook her head. 'I'm on retreat, Marco. I'm out of contact with everything familiar. It's the only way.'

His already pulverised heart whimpered. He suddenly pictured her far away from home, lonely and isolated, and falling in love with someone else. He couldn't bear the thought so instead of asking the question that burned him, he made it into a statement. 'You *will* come back.'

She rose on her toes and kissed him—a kiss filled with love and longing but devoid of a solid answer.

What was left of his heart splintered into a thousand pieces as she walked away.

* * *

Sweat poured off Marco as he lowered another fence post into position. He'd been out at Haven, repairing the yard in front of the old stables in preparation for the arrival of Ignacio's pony. Since Lucy had left he'd found that life went on and yet in so many ways it seemed to stop. For months he'd always thought the day he was granted permanent residency would be the day he started the next phase of his life. He would buy a dog, he would buy a property and polo horses. He now had official confirmation, but without Lucy everything seemed a pale imitation of itself and he'd done none of those things. He was living in limbo.

'Tea break.' William handed him a steaming mug.

He wiped his forehead with a bandana and accepted the tea. 'Beer would be better.'

'It's chilling for when we've earned it.' William raised his mug to him and surveyed their work. 'Another ten posts and we're done. Lucy won't believe it when she sees how well we've spruced it all up.'

Marco sighed. William always spoke of Lucy as if she was about to arrive any moment, but as each day passed, Marco found it harder to believe and he wanted more and more to jump on a plane, find her and bring her home. 'Why are you so convinced she is coming back?'

'I have to believe it. And so do you.' William clapped a hand on his shoulder. 'I'm sorry you're both suffering because of my mistake, but hold onto the fact she loves you. Loving someone is the easiest and hardest thing you'll ever do.'

'That I know.' He thought of his love for Ignacio which alternated between utter pride and heartache for his struggles. He remembered the exhilarating high of the moment he'd realised he loved Lucy and of the heartbreaking despair when she'd said she loved him but she had had to leave him. He was lonely with each long day that stretched out without her and the number of days she'd been absent were carved into his heart.

'Your love will bring her home.'

He put down his now empty mug. 'I am not so sure. She left because of me.'

'Exactly.'

'*Qué?*' He had no idea what William meant.

'I've never thanked you for writing to Lucy asking her to come to Bulla Creek. Duty brought her home but we both know we want her here with us because she wants to be here more than any other place. She needed to leave us for a while and as hard as it is, you did the right thing letting her go.'

William's hazel eyes urged him to keep the faith. 'She'll come back to Bulla Creek because of you as well.'

He thumped a fist into his palm. 'The moment she is back I am marrying her and *never* letting her leave again.'

The words tumbled out of him and with a brain-shuddering jolt he realised the idea of marriage no longer scared him. In fact, he'd never wanted anything more in his life than to be Lucy's husband.

William grinned at him. 'I'm glad you plan to marry her, but if she comes home she won't need a legal document to stay.' He cleared his throat. '*When* she comes home it will be for good.'

Marco had to believe that William was right.

CHAPTER TWELVE

Lucy purposely slipped on the plain, flat leather sandals she'd worn every day for three months and set out on the walk to the nearby tiny village. She hoped to buy some more paper—this time with lines on it because as it turned out, William had been correct. She couldn't draw to save herself, but she'd found she had a knack for words, something that she'd never really explored because she'd taken the science stream in high school.

During her first month in India, she hadn't ventured far from her self-imposed isolation. From the veranda outside her small room she was surrounded by towering, craggy mountains which made her feel almost insignificant and the rushing sound of racing water from the river relaxed her. Slowly, she'd managed to still her churning mind of the constant recriminations and regrets, the biggest one leaving Marco. It had taken a very long time for the question *Was coming here too much to ask of him?* to be silenced.

By the second month she'd found the calmness to try new things without any preconceived ideas or learned behaviours. She was an empty slate and she soaked up all her experiences. Now she had a sense of being herself rather than having been moulded into someone else. She hadn't worked as a doctor, or even thought of herself as one in weeks, which had freed her up and that had been when she'd realised she could write. Words had poured out of her and she'd written poetry, descriptive prose, short stories and letters. Lots of letters, although they remained tucked up in her satchel not posted and that was where they would remain. For the first time since she'd discovered she was adopted, she felt almost at peace with herself. The 'almost' was her stumbling block. She hadn't been able to make the final leap she'd expected to by now—the leap she'd watched others make.

She arrived at the village and stopped at the rough-hewn stall that made the best chai tea. She knew it was fresh because she could hear the ping of the milk being squeezed directly from the goat into the tin. She gave her order and sat down to wait.

The life of the village went on around her as she imagined it had for hundreds of years with cows wandering along the dusty street. A pedal-powered sewing machine whirred and brightly coloured material flashed in the sunlight. Lucy recognised 'wedding red' and smiled. Weddings were a multi-day affair where the actual marriage was just one part of the many ceremonies including the *mehndi* where the women decorated the bride and then each other with delicate henna designs.

Children dressed in very little were squatting down playing by the side of the road, looking for treasures that might have fallen off passing trucks. They called out to her and she waved back. A little boy crutched past toward the group, one of his legs withered and deformed, and unable to provide any support to him. Instantly, she thought of Ignacio. She'd worked hard on keeping all thoughts of home out of her mind but once she'd thought of him, he seemed to move right on in, snuggling down as if to say, *I've been waiting for you.*

She found herself comparing Iggie with the

Indian child. Even though his prematurity had caused his CP and his mother hadn't wanted him, he'd been lucky to be born to a father who could support him and love him.

Just like you.

Just like me.

She knew that now. Ruth and William loved her and even though Allison couldn't, their love was enough.

You didn't have to come to India to learn that. Marco told it to you weeks ago.

Her heart lurched as she thought about him. He'd been right but at the time she'd been unable to trust herself enough to know.

Her tea arrived as a truck rumbled past, throwing up dust to add to the millions of layers that preceded it. She automatically shielded the glass with her hand, wanting to enjoy the flavours of the chai spices not the dust. As she raised the drink to her lips, a child's pain-filled scream rent the air.

Terror froze her blood and the glass clattered against the table as she shot to her feet. After a rotation in paediatric emergency, she knew that harrowing sound too well, and nothing good ever came from it. She ran, following the gut-wrenching sound of women wailing and men yelling, and the first thing she saw was a broken crutch on the side of the road.

She lifted her gaze and just ahead of her she saw the little boy. He lay on the dirt and gravel of the road, his deformed leg in its normal alignment, but she could clearly see a white bone on his good leg protruding through the skin. The doctor inside her rushed back as she ran forward. Using her limited local language and hand actions, she explained who she was and started examining the child. She ruled out internal injuries and breathed more easily.

Compound fracture of the femur. Possible complications hypovolemic shock, fat embolism, osteomyleitis, bone shortening, avascular necrosis...

The diagnostic reel in her head ran on and her breath turned solid. In Australia this would be a serious injury but in rural India it was life-threatening. She ripped up the sarong she always carried in her bag and as she started bandaging, she sent up a prayer she could save this little boy and save his leg.

* * *

Twenty-four hours later Lucy was in a Delhi hospital having moved heaven and earth to get transport from the northern medical centre to bring him south, and then she'd done it all again to get him into surgery. That had been yesterday and now Arun lay between white sheets looking vulnerable and scared, but alive with a good chance of diminished complications. Today, she'd spoken to the surgeon and arranged for payment along with making sure Arun's mother had money so she could stay with him. Worried about the woman being alone in such a big city and so far from home, she'd contacted an Australian NGO and begged for follow-up for the family.

'We'll take it from here, Dr Patterson.' Jerry Tansy, from Aussies in India, smiled at her. 'You've done an amazing job.'

'Thank you, but it was just what anyone would have done.'

He didn't look so convinced. 'We could really do with someone like you on our team so if you're looking for a job in India…?'

She didn't have to think about the question. She'd spent hours fighting for her patient's life and for his ongoing care, and at four a.m., when

Arun had finally gone into surgery, she'd known without a shadow of a doubt that she was a doctor. Not because she'd been raised by William but because it was her passion and her vocation.

She was Lucy Patterson, doctor, and medicine ran in her veins.

Ran in her veins back in Bulla Creek where she belonged with the man and child she loved. India had given her space to work things out, but only Marco could fill the one gap in her quest for peace. Marco, Iggie and her loving father who'd given her so much—all of them had been with her in spirit the entire time she'd been in India, giving her love and support. Last night when she'd been saving Arun, it had been Marco's voice she'd heard guiding her and answering any clinical doubts.

It was time to go home.

What if he hasn't waited?

Time to find that out too.

She gave Jerry a weary smile. 'Thanks for the offer, but I've got a job and people I love and need back home.'

He pulled a business card out of his wallet. 'If

you change your mind or if there's anything I can
do to help just yell.'

'Do you have a phone I can use right now?'

'Sure.'

She accepted the mobile and moved into a quiet
alcove. With trembling fingers, she punched in
the number she knew off by heart. As she waited
for the connection, she could smell the clean
scent of eucalyptus, taste the strong flavours of
kangaroo and feel the wondrous feel of Marco's
arms around her as he buried his face in her hair.

The sound of the rings hummed in her ears for
nine long rings. *Please answer.*

The ringing stopped.

'Marco Rodriguez.'

His deep, accented voice came down the line
and her heart stuttered, and her throat tightened
as reality hit her that her future hung on this call.

Gripping the phone, she lifted her chin and
said, 'Marco, it's me.'

Lucy ran down the steps of the Fokker F50 and
straight into Marco's outstretched arms. Wrapping her arms around his neck, she kissed him

long and deep, as if he were the sole provider of desperately needed oxygen.

He broke the kiss and held her so tightly she could barely breathe and then he ran his hands over her hair and caressed her face with his fingers. 'I can't believe you're here.'

She half laughed and half cried. 'Believe it. I'm here and I'm never leaving again. At least not without you.'

He gazed at her, his eyes twinkling along with a myriad emotions. 'So it was worth it. You have learned something while you've been away.'

Her fingers curled into the placket of his shirt. 'I learned that you were right all along. Everything I need, want and love is right here in Bulla Creek. You...' She turned her head toward the low cyclone fence. 'Where are Ignacio and Dad?'

'Back at Haven. William suggested I meet you alone.'

A slow realisation washed over her. William had given them precious time together before they shared themselves with him and Ignacio. She smiled. 'I've also learned that my father is a very wise man.'

Marco smiled knowingly. 'He is. I don't think I

would have got through these three months without him, but he kept telling me to keep the faith and that you would come home to me and he was right.'

She bit her lip. 'Did you ever think loving me was too hard?'

'All the time and never.' He pressed a kiss to her forehead. 'Loving you is the joy of my life. You and Ignacio.'

'Oh, Marco.' Tears she'd long held back poured down her cheeks. 'I'm sorry I put us through all this but—'

'Shh.' He pressed a finger against her lips. 'There is no need to be sorry, I understand. Waiting was hard but it was important for you to go, and it has made us strong.' He stroked the tears away with the pad of his thumb. 'Lucy?'

She hiccoughed. 'Yes?'

Dark eyes stared down at her filled with love. 'Marry me.'

Joy surged and she threw her arms around his neck. 'Oh, Marco, you have no idea how I've longed to hear those words.'

He grinned. 'Is that a "yes"?'

'*Sí*, my darling Argentine, that is an emphatic

and categorical "yes". I will marry you and proudly be your wife and Iggie's mother.'

This time Marco's eyes seemed moist. 'You will be a wonderful mother to Ignacio because only you can truly understand the questions he will eventually ask about his mother.'

The thought of being a mum glowed deep down inside her. 'We'll be honest with him and help him through it together.'

He nodded his agreement. 'As his parents and as partners we will face whatever life throws at us. All that matters now is that you are home.'

She slid her arm around his waist as they walked to the car. 'So where is home?'

'William has offered to sell us Haven.'

Shocked surprise stilled her feet. 'Where would Dad go?'

Marco stroked her hair. 'He's talking about semi-retirement. Haven comes with twenty-five acres so if you are happy with the idea, he will build a house on the east side of the property and my parents will build on the west.'

'A family compound?' The idea circled around her, taking hold and reinforcing her feelings of true belonging. 'I like the idea.'

'So do I. We will fill it with children.'

'Fill?' She laughed. 'How about two or three brothers and sisters for Ignacio?'

'That sounds perfect.'

Holding her hand, he drove the short distance to his house and as he opened her door on the four-wheel-drive, she held out her arms. He stepped in and she gloried in the love and desire that burned so hot and strong in his eyes. With a wicked grin, she slowly slid down his body until her feet hit the ground. His heat and love seeped into her, bringing her body alive in a way it hadn't been in months, and it merged with his need and love until she thought she'd melt on the spot.

Groaning, he buried his face in her hair and then he cupped her buttocks and lifted her. She matched his groan with one of her own and wrapped her legs around his waist. 'God, I've missed you. Please take me home.'

'It will be my pleasure.' And he carried her inside to his bed.

A while later they lay under the soft touch of cotton sheets, nose to nose with their arms around each other.

Lucy gently pushed at Marco's shoulder until

he was on his back and then she straddled him, staring down into his eyes. 'You know you've got me for forever, right?'

'I do.' He pulled her down against him, kissing her long and hard, and infusing her with his love and ever-lasting commitment.

EPILOGUE

'Mum, I like it when you're *this* pregnant.'

Startled, Lucy pushed herself up slowly from the vegetable crisper and closed the fridge door, not even trying to second-guess what made her very bright ten-year-old son say that.

At eight and a half months pregnant, Lucy was thinking that as much as she enjoyed being pregnant, she was ready to hold this baby in her arms. 'That makes one of us, Iggie. Why?'

He grinned. 'Because for a little while. I'm not the slowest walker in the family. Even when you go fast. You waddle.'

Laughing, she threw a carrot at him and he caught it with an even bigger grin. Her heart swelled at how much his hand-eye co-ordination and balance had improved over the years and at how hard he worked at it.

'Take that and some apples, and go feed Hoola and Hooper before I waddle after you and make you dry the dishes. Take your sister with you, please.'

'Okay. Come on, Ruthie, let's go feed the horseys.' He held out his hand to his four-year-old sister who happily took it and skipped along next to his loping gait.

Two minutes after they'd left, the wire door banged open and William walked in first, holding flowers and wine, immediately followed by Ana and Carlos, Marco's parents. They immediately started fussing.

'Lucy, why are you on your feet?' William asked, looking concerned. 'You worked this morning so you're supposed to be taking it easy. Any twinges?'

'We stay and we cook the dinner. It is ready at seven,' Ana added, strapping on an apron.

Carlos tapped the cooler he'd carried in. 'Steak. Is good for the *bebé*.'

Lucy held up her hands in mock surrender. 'I was making a salad, but I can easily stop and go and sit on the veranda, and catch the breeze.'

'You do that,' her father instructed. 'Leave the kids and the dinner to us. All you have to do is be at the table in an hour.'

'Iggie and Ruth are feeding the horses and then the dogs. Dad, can you check on them?'

'Sure. I know the drill and I'll bath Ruthie. Now go.'

She let herself be shooed outside and just as she was about to sit down she heard the crunch of gravel under car tyres. She met Marco at the bottom of the steps. With some flecks of silver nestling in his jet-black hair, she thought he was even more handsome than when she'd met him five years ago.

The most rewarding and wonderful five years of her life. Not that there hadn't been challenges, but Marco's prediction had been correct. They both knew the pain of being apart which made them work even harder at being together and making their family a happy one.

He slipped his arms around her waist and bent in to kiss her before dropping a kiss on her swollen belly.

She kissed him back. 'It's Friday night and everyone's here. The grandparents are busy being helpful.'

A hopeful expression lit across his face. 'That means steak for dinner?'

'It does. It also means you get a glass of wine because William's on call and no dishes for either of us. We're being very spoiled.'

She felt spoiled all of the time. Marco adored her, William took his role as a grandfather very seriously and Marco's parents, who spent half the year in Australia and other half in Argentina, had reorganised their schedule to be here for the birth of their third grandchild. For someone who'd once thought she had no family, she now had it in spades.

She ran her fingers along Marco's chest, loving the feel of him under her fingers, a feeling that had only grown over time. 'Iggie says I waddle.'

He smiled down at her. '*Sí*, you do.'

She gave him a gentle punch. 'That's not helping. I'm feeling fat and frumpy and I'm sick of patients saying, "I thought you'd have had the baby by now".'

'Come.' He held out his hand and walked her to veranda swing and they sat down. 'You are beautiful.'

She dropped her head on his shoulder, snuggling in. 'Go on.'

His hand caressed her shoulder. 'You glow with an aura of fecundity that is very sexy.'

She wriggled her nose. 'Really?'

'Yes.' He gave her a long, open-mouthed kiss and her body immediately went slack.

'Hmm, you'll have to kiss me like that again after dinner.'

His eyes darkened with a wicked glint. 'Didn't you say the grandparents were on duty?'

'I did. But you're a boring, old married man so you can't possibly be suggesting—'

'You cannot call the Bulla Creek Polo champion old.' He pulled her to her feet and started walking softly around the veranda toward the front of the house and their room.

She grinned. 'I can if you say I waddle.'

He opened the French doors and tugged her into their bedroom, closing the curtains behind him. Pressing his lips to her neck, he started a delicious trail of kisses. 'You glide like a swan.'

She let her head fall back. 'Now you're talking.'

Only he'd stopped talking and she didn't mind one little bit.

* * * * *

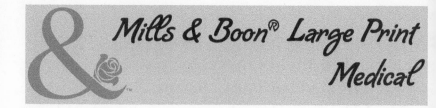
Mills & Boon® Large Print Medical